JULIE ANDERSON felt like a fool. She was hopelessly in love with the irresponsible Doug, but she was already engaged to another man. Would her heart betray her again?

KIM DOUGLAS was thrilled that Doug wanted her—until she found she was just a pawn in his game to win Julie. But Doug had miscalculated. He didn't know that Kim played for keeps.

MICKEY HORTON meticulously plotted the deaths of Bill and Laura. They would pay for committing him to Bayview Sanitarium. Since Laura had foolishly agreed to be his therapist, his task would be so easy. . . .

Author **Marcia Lawrence** has lived most of her life in the Pacific Northwest. A mother of two children, she writes when she's not making trips to soccer games and the dentist.

From the editor's desk...

Dear Friend,

Captivating . . . exciting . . . heartwarming! These are but a few of the comments we've received from Soaps & Serials readers. We're delighted. Every month the fine writers and editors at Pioneer pool all their resources to bring you brand-new spectacular books.

Based on actual scripts from DAYS OF OUR LIVES, each novel is written with you in mind. Soaps & Serials take you back to the very beginning of the show, revealing the innocent and infamous pasts of your favorite characters, recreating cherished moments from your favorite episodes. And though each book is a complete, satisfying read, our sensational cliffhanger ending is just a hint of the drama that will unfold in next month's Soaps & Serials book.

We receive numerous requests for previous volumes of Soaps & Serials. If you are also curious about how it all began—or if you want to complete your collection— please see the order form inserted in this book.

For Soaps & Serials,

Rosalind Noonan

Rosalind Noonan
Editor-in-Chief
Pioneer Communications Network, Inc.

DAYS OF OUR LIVES

14

OBSESSIONS

Soaps & Serials™

PIONEER COMMUNICATIONS NETWORK, INC.

Obsessions

ISBN: 1-55726-153-9

Printed in Canada

10 9 8 7 6 5 4 3 2 1

Between the Lines

One of the most intriguing romantic triangles ever featured on DAYS OF OUR LIVES involved the characters of Laura, Mickey, and Bill Horton. As the Horton brothers battle over Laura, Bill fears for his life. Ed Mallory, the actor who played Dr. Bill Horton during this tumultuous period, also encountered a dangerous situation off-camera.

An earthquake hit his San Fernando Valley home, sending furniture and fixtures flying in all directions. The crib carrying Ed's infant son was tossed around the bedroom. Miraculously, Ed guided his family to safety, but not before he fell onto a glass-topped table, injuring his leg.

Carrying on the age-old tradition that the show must go on, Ed appeared at the studio minutes before air time. Since his leg was still bleeding, however, the NBC cameras could film him only from the waist up!

Chapter One
Out of Touch

"Now I'm going to get you. . . ." Mickey Horton whispered, his eyes gleaming with vengeance in the dark room. Just as he hoped, his weapon fell into his open hands. "Okay, big brother!" Though he was alone, he could imagine the shock in Bill's eyes when he got even.

For the past two hours he'd worked on the corner of the closet mirror in his room at Bayview Sanitarium. The metal framing the mirror had finally bent, and he'd broken off a long shard of glass. Small enough to conceal, it was sharp and deadly. "Perfect! You're all mine, Bill," he whispered. "You and that lying, cheating wife of yours!"

Heart pounding, he sneaked back to his bed and flopped down onto the hard, springless mattress. He propped his pillow up to support his head, glanced around the room and searched for a hiding place for the makeshift knife.

There was none. Everything in Mickey's room was either bolted down or harmless: perfectly safe for the patients.

"Great," he muttered, fingering the sharp glass. There had to be someplace—a hiding spot that the guards wouldn't find in one of their surprise searches. *Come on, Mickey. You just have to be smarter than they are.*

He glanced at the small sink and toilet. Then he got up and turned on the faucet. Splashing water on his face, he looked for nooks and crannies around the steel pipes. Nothing!

"Damn." He bit his tongue, glancing at the dark two-way mirror on the wall across from the bed. The guards were probably still watching him. Damn the whole lot of them, and the Horton family—*his* family—for committing him! *Come on, Mickey, think! You're smarter than they are. All of them—including Bill!*

Sweating, he glanced back at the closet, where the door still hung open.

"Bingo," he whispered.

The closet was the one dead spot in the guards' viewing area. He slipped behind the open door and, without a second thought, bent the thin metal molding around the edge of the mirror. The broken shard slipped back into place.

The crack in the glass was almost invisible!

Now, anytime he needed a weapon, he had one. A quick pull on the molding, and the crudely fashioned, knife-shaped piece of glass would fall into his hands.

He slipped back into bed and smiled coldly as he stared up at the ceiling. All he had to do was wait.

Linda Phillips sipped her coffee and stared through her kitchen window. A blanket of snow gleamed white under the streetlights as dawn began to brighten the pitch-dark sky.

"Oh, Mickey," she whispered, then glanced at the table where her daughter squirmed in her chair.

"I want syrup," Melissa said, pursing her lips and tossing her blond curls defiantly.

"We're out of syrup. Use jam."

"Don't like jam!" The four-year-old rubbed her eyes and yawned. Still clinging to an old doll and a tattered blanket, Melissa was barely awake.

Linda sighed and smiled at her child. "Come on, honey. Let's not argue. Not this morning. Mommy's got to be at work early. You remember about Mommy's new job with Mr. Quinn?"

Melissa wasn't interested. "Want syrup!" she repeated.

"Tomorrow, you can have syrup, but today you eat your pancakes with jam." Linda began spreading strawberry jam over the two uneaten pancakes, but Melissa kicked her chair back from the table and ran out of the room.

"You come back here this minute!" Linda called after her, then sighed, knowing the effort was useless. Ever since her father's death, Melissa had been hard to handle.

Linda was worried. Maybe Melissa needed to see a psychiatrist.

"Yeah, like Laura Horton," she drawled sarcastically as she threw Melissa's rejected pancakes into the sink. At the thought of Mickey's ex-wife, Linda seethed inside. She pushed her blond hair out of her eyes. The fact that Laura had eventually wound up marrying Mickey's brother, Bill, made Linda feel sick. She finished her coffee, poured the dregs down the sink and tried not to think about Laura or Bill or any of that miserable Horton clan.

"Get dressed, now, okay?" she called down the hall.

"I am!"

"What the child needs is a father!" Linda muttered angrily as she swept the pancakes into the disposal. "A father like Mickey Horton!" Ever since Mickey's sanity hearing and subsequent commitment to Bayview Sanitarium, Linda had been a wreck. She felt that the Horton family had railroaded him with their damaging testimony.

Sighing, she walked to her bedroom. "Don't worry, darling," she whispered, as if Mickey were in the room with her. "I'll get you out. I don't know how, but I will." Untying her robe, she looked at her battered old dresser, where she still kept a framed snapshot of Mickey. It had been taken several years ago, when she had been involved with him. Wearing shorts and a lopsided grin, he smiled into the camera, his sensuous blue eyes sparkling at some private joke.

· But that had been a long time ago—before he'd lost his memory and married that farmgirl, Maggie!

Linda smiled. Now, for the first time in years, she had a real chance to win him back. His amnesia was gone, his memory had returned completely. Maybe some of the old flames still burned and he would fall in love with her again. But first, she had to get him out of that horrid mental institution.

"Hurry up, Melissa," she called through the thin wall. "We don't want to be late for nursery school."

"I'm getting dressed!"

"Good. Me, too." Linda tossed her robe on the foot of the bed and headed for the shower.

Within an hour, she was unlocking the doors of Alan Quinn's law office. "Five minutes early," she said, pleased, as she took off her coat, hung it on a brass coat tree and glanced around her new workplace. The desks and chairs were modern, of heavy oak and chrome. Watercolors hung on the cream-colored walls, and the big windows let in plenty of pale winter light. "A far cry from Don Craig's stuffy offices," she murmured, glancing around the rooms. Yes, she was going to like working here, she decided, and Alan, whether he knew it or not, was going to help her free Mickey!

Humming to herself, she made a pot of coffee, then tackled a large stack of depositions that had to be copied and collated. She was nearly finished when she heard the door open.

Alan Quinn, tall and slim with thinning blond hair, was unwrapping a wool scarf from around his neck. He glanced in her direction and nodded. "Good morning."

She looked up and smiled. "Hi."

"Hard at work already, I see."

"Just trying to make a good impression on my new boss," Linda answered lightly.

"Well, you are."

Thank God! Linda's smile widened. She needed to impress Alan, get him on her side, so that he would help her. "I wanted to get everything organized early today."

"Good."

Carrying the depositions to his office, she placed them on the long credenza behind his desk, then offered him a cup of coffee.

"Thanks."

"You look like you're on top of the world," she said.

"I guess I am." He flashed her a quick smile. "I don't know why, but I feel great. Maybe it's the new secretary I hired."

"I doubt it."

He snapped open his briefcase and pulled out a sheaf of hand-scrawled notes. "Do you ever get the feeling that everything you do is going to come out right?"

Never! Linda's brows puckered. " 'Fraid not. Lately, I feel like everything I touch is turning to rust."

"Oh, come on, Linda. Things can't be that bad."

"Well, maybe not. . . ."

Alan saw the worry in her eyes. "Want to talk about it?" he asked, glancing at his watch. "We've got a few minutes."

"I don't know."

"Why not? We're going to be working together. It can't hurt to clear the air."

"Maybe you're right." Linda poured herself a cup of coffee from the carafe on his desk and sank into a leather chair near the window. Why not confide in him? What would it hurt?

"It's about Mickey Horton, isn't it?" he guessed.

Startled, she glanced up. "How did you know?"

Alan hooked a leg over the corner of his desk and sipped his coffee. "It was pretty obvious at his sanity hearing."

"Obvious?"

"The way you feel about him," Alan said. "And, after all, you were the one who tried to hire me to help him—that was before you knew that he planned to defend himself."

"I . . . I just wanted to help. He's an old friend."

"More than that, I'd guess. So, go on, tell me about it. And the Horton family?" he said, his lips curving downward. "You looked like you wanted to strangle every last one of them!"

"I did," she admitted, grimacing as she remembered how the entire Horton clan had trooped sanctimoniously into the courtroom just to condemn him. "I can't believe how they all worked to get him! Even Tom. His own father, Salem's favorite doctor and saint, as good as slammed the door on him! Mickey must have been devastated to have been betrayed like that."

"Probably."

Linda was still fuming. "And that no-good, Don Craig."

"Careful now, you worked for him." There was a spark of amusement in Alan's cold eyes.

"Don't remind me," she murmured glumly, remembering Don's arguments at the hearing. "I could see the glee written all over his face when Mickey was sentenced! And do you know why? Because he's been living fat off Mickey's old clients. I can't believe he can look himself in the mirror," Linda said, angry all over again.

"Don had to take the position that he did. He was representing Tom," Alan pointed out, enjoying the part of devil's advocate.

"Hmmph!"

"And Don probably didn't want to see Mickey put away—"

"Like hell!" Linda snapped.

"Look, it was his job."

"Well, he didn't have to do it with such . . . such fervor!"

"But the family was trying to help Mickey."

"*Help* him?" she repeated bitterly. "They only wanted to shuffle him out of their lives in order to protect Bill and Laura. Did you know that while Laura was married to Mickey, she had an affair with Bill—and that Michael, the boy Mickey always thought was his son, is really Bill's child?"

"I heard that at the hearing—and it wasn't really an affair. More like a one-night stand, according to Bill."

"Do you believe that?"

Alan lifted a shoulder. "Doesn't matter what I believe."

Linda was so furious she was beginning to shake. "All these years Bill and Laura have hidden the truth from Mickey and their son, just so they could look respectable. And Tom was in on it, too! He *knew* Bill was Michael's father! How can you even think that anyone in that family cares about Mickey?"

"Mickey's family is trying to help him the only way they know how, I suppose," Alan said. "They were trying to protect him."

"By sending him to Bayview?" She set her cup on the desk and stood. Her eyes had turned a vengeful shade of blue. "I guess my idea of what's best for Mickey is a lot different from theirs. He should be out of that place and with people who love him."

"Meaning you—or his wife, Maggie?"

That country bumpkin? Linda thought. *The farm girl?* "Wherever he feels the most comfortable," she said, not meeting his eyes.

"Maybe this isn't your problem, Linda. He does have a family and a wife," Alan pointed out.

"I've made it my problem!"

"Because you love him."

"Yes," she whispered desperately. "Alan, please! You've got to help me find a way to get Mickey out of that horrible place!"

"I don't know—"

"Please!" Linda repeated, seeing a flicker of interest in his eyes. "You've got an idea, don't you?"

"I don't know yet." He crossed the room to the bookcase on the far wall. Pulling out one of the old, leather-bound volumes, he started leafing through it, then suddenly stopped, absorbed in what he'd found.

"What is it?"

He looked up, his flinty gray eyes calculating. "I think this is probably what you had in mind."

"What?" Her heart leaped. There was a way!

"It's simple, really. The laws of this state are designed to protect the rights of individuals—all individuals. Even those who are suspected of being insane."

"I don't follow you."

"For example, if an individual is institutionalized against his will—"

"Like Mickey!"

"Yes. There's a habeas corpus law that allows him to petition a higher court to hear his case."

Linda's mouth curved upward. "That means he can get out of there, right?"

"Maybe." Alan placed the open book on the desk. "What he can do is present his case before the state's superior court. I don't know if they'd overturn Judge Gelson's decision, but at least Mickey has a chance. If that's what he wants to do."

"Of course it's what he wants!" Linda said ecstatically, scanning the statute.

"And I suppose you'd like to tell him?"

"Oh, yes!"

"Then why don't you?" he suggested. "I need you to get some things out for me this morning, but for the rest of the day I'll be in court. So, if you leave here right after lunch, I suppose you'd have plenty of time to get to Bayview."

Linda could hardly believe her good luck. She beamed at her boss. "Thanks, Alan. You're the greatest! I promise I'll get everything done this morning, and I'll be in tomorrow morning bright and early."

True to her word, Linda got all the necessary work done and on Alan's desk by noon. She made a photocopy of the statute protecting Mickey's rights; then, grabbing her coat and purse, she ran out the door, waited impatiently for the elevator, got out at the parking level and climbed into her car. Now she could start winning Mickey back!

Maggie Horton shivered as she hurried up the sidewalk toward the two-story apartment building. The snow had been shoveled off the cracked cement, but a thick white mantle still covered the ground. Two old maple trees, now leafless and stark, stood guard near the front door of the gray building. Maggie eyed the place, and then thought about her husband locked away, out of touch with the world.

"Oh, Mickey, how could this have happened?" she wondered aloud. "Everything was perfect, and now. . . ." She shuddered, watching her breath crystallize in the freezing air. Now Mickey was locked up like a common criminal!

Since the night of Michael's accident on the farm, the night when the hay wagon had slipped and fallen on the boy, everything in Maggie's life had been turned upside down. Not only had Michael had to battle for his life in Brookville Hospital, but Mickey had discovered that Michael wasn't really his son. That was when Mickey's amnesia had completely disappeared and his fragile grasp on reality had snapped.

His life as Marty Hansen had dissolved into nothing, and he'd remembered with blinding clarity every detail of his life as Mickey Horton—including the fact that nearly everyone in his family had lied to him. Anger and hatred had consumed him; he'd turned into a monster Maggie didn't recognize. And in the turmoil of his emotions, he'd forgotten Maggie and all that they had shared.

She looked down at her left hand, at the gold band on her ring finger, and a single tear slid down her face as she climbed the two steps to the manager's apartment. Then, brushing the tear away and stiffening her spine, she rang the bell.

A middle-aged, redheaded woman cracked open the door. "What d'ya want?"

Maggie held up the newspaper she'd tucked under her arm. "Do you have a room for rent?"

"One. It's upstairs, 'round back."

"Could I see it, please?"

The large woman looked Maggie up and down, then opened the door wider. "Sure. Molly Ferguson's the name." She plucked a large key ring off a wooden peg on the wall, came outside, and slammed the door shut behind her. "Follow me."

"I'm Maggie Horton."

"Horton? You mean you're related to that guy who tried to kill his brother and ended up at Bayview? I read about it in the papers."

"He didn't try to kill anyone!" Maggie said angrily, tired of the personal questions that had been tossed at her like poisoned spears over the past few days. She forced her voice back to calmness. "Mickey is my husband. He . . . he just suffered a nervous break-down and needs a little rest. That's all."

"If you say so."

Maggie, following Molly through the snow, changed the subject. "This is the closest apartment building to Bayview Sanitarium, isn't it?"

Molly chose to ignore the brand-new units on the other side of the freeway. "Sure is."

"Good. I want to be as close to the hospi-tal as possible. We—Mickey and I—live out-side of Brookville on a farm and I can't come here every day, so I thought I'd better get an apartment close to the hospital—just for a couple of months or so."

Molly unlocked the door and sized Maggie up, then gave her a gap-toothed smile. With her fresh-scrubbed face, neatly combed red-brown hair and sincere smile, Maggie Horton looked as honest as the day was long. Too bad she'd hooked herself up with a loony like Mickey Horton, Molly thought. "I'll need the rent up front," she said, trudging up a stairway to the second-story unit. "This room's been vacant awhile."

As soon as Maggie walked in the door she was assaulted by the odor of stale air, mothballs and disinfectant. Holding her breath, she listened while Molly opened the windows and rambled on about the merits of the long-vacant unit. Frigid air rushed into the room.

Maggie eyed the place. Fortunately, the small apartment was furnished with a daybed, a table, two chairs and a small refrigerator and stove. Now, if the price was right . . .

"A hundred and ten a month," Molly said, crossing her arms over her ample bosom.

A lot of money, Maggie thought, but worth the price, to be near Mickey. "I'll take it. But I'll need to have a phone installed. I own a farm in Brookville, and I need to keep in touch with my hired hands."

"Just so long as you don't skip out and leave me with the long-distance charges."

"You can count on me."

"Good."

Maggie wrote a check and handed it to the older woman. After studying the piece of paper, Molly pushed it into the pocket of her jacket and handed Maggie a key. "Let me know if ya need anything," she said, and closed the door behind her.

"All I need is my husband back," Maggie whispered. She walked over to the kitchen sink and looked through the grimy window-panes. In the distance, high on a snow-covered hill, stood the gray fortress of Bayview Sanitarium.

The east wind blowing off Lake Michigan sliced through Doug Williams like a razor. With the collar of his fleece-lined jacket turned up, he climbed into a cab to make his daily trek out to the airport to check on weather conditions.

He'd been stuck in Chicago for more than a week—nearly two weeks by now—and it was driving him crazy. All he wanted to do was return to Salem and Julie Anderson.

He felt a little warmer when he thought of Julie, of her long brown hair, trusting blue eyes and easy smile. Before he'd left Salem, they'd had a major argument, for which he'd been as much to blame as she. Now, he could barely remember what the argument had been about, although he knew it had something to do with Kim, his ex-wife.

He closed his eyes and leaned back against the cab's shiny upholstery. He'd tried to call Julie several times since landing in Chicago, but had never gotten through.

"Where to, buddy?" the cabbie asked as he punched the meter.

"O'Hare."

"Ha! You thinkin' about takin' a trip in this weather?" The cab slid slightly on the icy street as the driver eased into the heavy traffic in front of the Town Center Hotel.

"I've got to get home."

"If I were you, I'd relax," the cabbie advised. "Enjoy Chicago."

"Doesn't look like I'll have much of a choice," Doug said, his mouth twisting downward as he eyed the gray sky and the snow and sleet collecting on the windshield.

The airport had been closed for all but a few hours during the last four days. Telephones and electricity in the Midwest had been at the mercy of the weather and repair crews.

Stranded and out of touch, Doug had grown more impatient with each passing hour.

"So what're ya doin' in Chicago?" the driver asked.

"You wouldn't believe me if I told you."

"Try me." The cabbie glanced in the mirror; the look in his eyes said he'd heard it all before.

"I came to make sure that the divorce I thought was final, really was."

"Your ex tryin' to hit you up for alimony?"

More like blackmail, Doug thought. "Nope. She lied. Told me we were still married."

"And you believed her?"

How would I know? I was in prison when the divorce went through. "I wasn't sure."

"No papers, huh?"

"Nope. I was away from home when it was supposed to have been final."

"So she lied to you?" the cabdriver asked, lighting a cigarette and squinting through the smoke. "Wouldn't ya know!"

Doug's lips curved cynically as he thought about Kim. She'd been trying to break up his relationship with Julie from the minute she'd set foot in Salem. Still, he couldn't really hate her. Though he'd tried to despise her for all the trouble she'd caused, he still cared for her. Worse still, Hope, his daughter from his second marriage, had taken to Kim instantly; the little girl worshipped the ground Kim walked on. "Kim's okay," he said finally, glancing out the window.

"Sure, sure. Sounds like a real charmer. If ya ask me, you should give her her walking papers, and quick!"

"I guess I have." A copy of the divorce decree was burning a hole in his pocket. He couldn't wait to show it to Julie. Finally he was a free man. Well, actually, he always had been; Kim had just been blowing smoke, and he should never have believed her. But he had to hand it to her, she'd played her cards just right, only confessing the truth about the divorce when she'd caught up with him on the courthouse steps a few days ago.

By then he hadn't believed a word she'd said. Doug had demanded proof of the divorce and had gotten it in the courthouse.

Then, just when he'd thought he was home free, the storm had hit Chicago. Weathermen had been calling it the worst storm in half a century. Travel had been impossible. Frustrated, Doug had sat in his hotel room and waited in a fever of impatience to get back to Julie.

The taxi, arriving at the airport, slid around several parked cars. "Here ya go," the cabbie said. "Nice talkin' to ya."

"Sure." Doug paid his fare, and entered the terminal.

O'Hare was a madhouse. The airport was crawling with people. Thousands of stranded passengers had camped out within the giant terminal structure. Benches, chairs, and tables had been converted into living quarters and beds. Children cried and whined; older people tried to sleep wherever they could find a spot.

Doug stood in line after line, hoping to find a plane to get him out of the city. But the airport was still completely shut down, and after three hours, he once again gave up hope of getting out of Chicago in the near future.

Exasperated, he found a pay phone and dialed Julie's number, listening to the phone ring unanswered on the other end. "Come on, Julie. Where are you?" he muttered.

Finally he slammed the receiver into the cradle, then lifted it again and punched out Alice and Tom Horton's number. His daughter, Hope, had been staying with her grandparents, and Doug was worried. Not only had he read about the explosion at the Syntron Chemical plant in Salem, but a couple days later the newspaper had reported that Mickey Horton had been found insane and placed in a sanitarium. It seemed as if the entire town of Salem had fallen apart since he'd left.

A busy signal beeped in his ear and he hung up, feeling totally isolated. Shoving his hands into his pockets, he walked to one of the large plate-glass windows overlooking the tarmac. Through the glass he could see the huge planes, idle on the runway, ice and snow covering their wings and fuselages, and he knew it would be days before he could get back to Salem.

"Wonderful," he muttered. "Just wonderful."

Feeling as if he were merely spinning his wheels, he walked outside and took a cab back to his hotel. "Home sweet home," he mocked, pushing open the glass doors and heading for the elevators.

Upstairs, he was just unlocking his door when Kim poked her head into the hallway.

"Got a minute for an old friend?" she asked.

The corner of his mouth twitched upward. He was bored stiff, and he couldn't see that talking to her would hurt anything. "Sure, come on in."

"Beautiful day, huh?" she said, watching Doug wander over to stare out the window at the gray skies and the sleet slanting on the glass.

"Just great."

She sat in one of the two chairs and tucked her legs beneath her, her long, ebony hair hanging to her waist. She licked her lips, and her dark eyes gazed thoughtfully at Doug. She knew what she had to do was going to be difficult. At first she'd only wanted Doug for his money, the money he'd inherited from his second wife, Addie. But some of the old sparks between them had rekindled, and now Kim had realized that she had actually fallen in love with him all over again.

"I'm so bored I can't stand it," she remarked casually. "I've seen so much TV that my eyes are rectangular, and I've read every magazine they carry at that stupid newsstand, including some weird publication called *Mother Earth News*. I'm going crazy."

"I know what you mean."

Kim glanced up at him and swallowed. If only he would look at her. But he didn't move and his face seemed to be set in stone. "Doug?"

"Yeah?"

"I just wanted to talk to you one last time before you get out of here and go back to Salem. I want you to know why I lied to you—"

"You don't have to explain," he interrupted.

"But I want to! Really!"

He looked at her then, his blue eyes unreadable. "Why?"

"Because I've done some pretty rotten things."

"I can't argue with that."

"But there's a reason. I only did them because I still love you."

"I don't want to hear this."

"But you have to! Don't you understand? I didn't want to foul up your life, not with Julie or your friends. I just wanted to be a part of it."

"And you thought you could accomplish that by lying to me and Julie, by manipulating us both, by parking yourself in my house, by claiming that we were still married and that we had to stay married so that you could get your inheritance?"

"Y-yes," she whispered, looking up at him through a sheen of tears. "I don't blame you for being mad."

"Good." He propped one shoulder against the wall and told himself not to be taken in by her act; she'd lied too much in the past. But she looked so damned innocent and miserable that it was hard to remember what a cunning fox she really was.

"I'm sorry, Doug."

"It's over. Forget it."

"It's just that I would have done anything to get you back."

Doug felt like an absolute jerk. "Look, I'm not blind. I know you didn't mean to hurt me. You just never realized how much I love Julie."

"She's one lucky lady."

"Nope." He smiled crookedly, and Kim's heart twisted. "I'm one lucky guy."

"Then I guess I'd better go," Kim whispered, standing and brushing away her tears. "I'll see you later."

"Sure."

As she left, Doug reached for the phone. He *had* to get through to Julie. Lying back on the bed, he listened as the line connected, picturing Julie, with her bright eyes and dimpled smile, in his mind. He let it ring twenty times before finally hanging up.

So, where was she? Doug ran a hand over his chin and his eyes narrowed. And with whom?

Chapter Two
Rage

Julie picked up the phone in her son's room, listened for a second and then hung up. "I guess you're right," she said, frowning.

"I told ya," David said. "No one can call in and we can't call out."

"And you're bored out of your mind," she said, smiling at him.

"I don't like being cooped up."

"I know." She looked at the bandage still swathing David's head. His unruly dark hair poked out from beneath the white gauze. "But Grandpa said to stay off your feet for at least a week. A concussion's nothing to fool around with."

"I know," David grumbled, shifting in the bed. "I just don't understand why the phone's not working."

"From what I understand, crews are working around the clock. We're lucky even to have electricity. With the storm coming on the heels of that explosion—"

"I know, I know," David said.

"Nothing on TV, huh?"

"Reruns, game shows and soap operas." He looked up at her with soulful brown eyes. "If I could just call Paul Grant, maybe he could stop by."

"You're very close to him, aren't you?" Julie asked, remembering the kind black man who had visited David in the hospital.

"He saved my life," David admitted, glancing out the window. "Took me in when I needed a place to stay." He shifted on the bed. He was never comfortable talking about the months during which he'd disappeared from Salem after driving off the Kelley Point Bridge. For a long time he'd let Julie think he was dead, and it still bothered him.

"Would you like me to ask him to stop by?" she said. "I could drive over there."

"Naw. Forget it. Maybe I'd better just try to sleep so I can get out of this bed."

"Maybe." She snapped off his bedside lamp. Afternoon light still reflected from the snow outside the window to stream through the glass and warm the room. "Enjoy your time off."

"I don't have much choice, do I?"

Julie smiled to herself. David wanted to get up, and that was a good sign. At least he was feeling better. Shutting his door, she walked into the living room and stopped at the piano, her smile fading. There, on the polished wooden surface, was a picture of Doug, his arm slung familiarly around her shoulders.

Though it had been taken only last summer, it now seemed like a lifetime since Tom had snapped the shot. Now Doug was in Chicago—with his wife, Kim, the wife he hadn't bothered mentioning to Julie. Suddenly close to tears, she picked up the picture and shoved it into the nearest drawer. Her life with Doug was over and she didn't want any reminders of the time they'd shared.

But he was going to Chicago to make sure the divorce was final—remember? an inner voice reminded her. Frowning, she chased away her lingering feelings of love. He'd gone to Chicago with Kim. And he hadn't even bothered to call! *He can't. The phones are out.*

"I can't stand it!" she muttered, tormented by doubts. She'd loved Doug for so long that it was hard to chase him out of her mind. Grabbing her coat, she went outside for a walk, determined to forget Doug forever. But the tears wouldn't go away.

It was midafternoon when Linda Phillips pulled into the parking lot at Bayview Sanitarium. She was scarcely able to conceal her excitement. Finally, she could help Mickey!

Stepping out of the car, she bent her head against a blast of frigid winter air. "God, it's cold," she muttered, breaking into a trot, her heels sliding on the patches of ice as she hurried to the main doors and ducked inside.

"May I help you?" asked the woman behind the large window at the front desk.

With her wire-rimmed glasses and her gray hair pulled back in a tight bun, the nurse looked as severe as the hospital itself.

"Yes. I'd like to see Mickey Horton, please."

"Mickey Horton," the nurse repeated, glancing at the register. "Are you a member of the immediate family?"

Linda was tempted to lie but didn't. "No, just a very close friend."

"I'm afraid it's not the usual visiting time, Ms. . . . ?"

"Phillips. Linda Phillips," she answered, trying to hide her annoyance. "It's really important that I see Mickey."

"If you could tell me the nature of your visit, I will call Dr. Powell and clear it with him, if possible."

"As I said, I'm a very close friend of Mickey's, and I have important legal information concerning his case. He asked me to keep him informed on any developments that occurred."

"Legal information?" Dubiously the nurse called Dr. Powell. Linda waited on pins and needles, unable to hear what was being said behind the glass partition.

Finally, the nurse hung up. "Dr. Powell says that you may see Mr. Horton, but it has to be a restricted visit."

"What's that?"

"You'll have two staff members in the room with you at all times."

"But—"

"And you can only visit for fifteen minutes."

"Fifteen minutes?" Linda repeated incredulously. "But I came all the way from Salem. That's not nearly enough—"

"And one of the orderlies will ask you to leave if Mr. Horton shows any signs of distress. Now, I must ask you to check your purse here at the desk."

Rolling her eyes heavenward, Linda wondered whether she was going to be strip-searched, but she held her tongue and didn't complain. The important thing was to get him out, she told herself as she waited for the orderlies to show her to Mickey's room.

A few minutes later, she was escorted through a locked door and following two tall orderlies down a long hallway. They stopped at room 115, unlocked the door, and Linda walked into the room.

When she saw Mickey, her heart wrenched. His sandy-colored hair unkempt, his chin darkened by a stubble of beard, he was sitting slumped on the edge of his bed. He didn't even look up.

"Mr. Horton, you have a visitor," the lanky orderly said.

Mickey didn't move. He just stared across the room and muttered something under his breath.

"Mickey?" Linda whispered, stepping closer.

No response.

"Mickey, it's Linda."

When he didn't move, she turned to the orderlies. "Can't he hear me?"

The hefty one lifted a shoulder. "Who knows?"

Linda wasn't about to be deterred. She walked over to the bed, and knelt down. "Oh, Mickey. How are you?"

Without glancing up, he continued his mumbled chant. "Miserable nurses . . . spying nurses . . . just go away."

"What?" She turned again to the orderlies, who were leaning against the wall near the door. "What's he talking about?"

"Who knows? Ask him."

"Mickey?" Linda tried to focus his attention on her face by touching his chin and looking directly into his blank eyes. "Mickey, it's me, Linda. Linda Phillips. I'm not a nurse. I'm your friend."

A faint glimmer of recognition lit his eyes, and his lips twitched. "Linda . . . Phillips?"

"Yes! Yes! Linda!" She was so relieved that she wanted to cry.

Mickey smiled a little. At least, Linda thought it was a smile. "Sit down, Linda," he said finally.

"I've been so worried about you!"

"Is that why you came to see me?"

"Oh, yes. And to get you out of this awful place!" She sat beside him on the corner of the bed.

"How?"

Excitedly she told him about her talk with Alan Quinn and the statute that might be his ticket to freedom.

The orderlies were bored; they'd heard it all before. Seeing that Mickey was accepting his visitor calmly, they ignored the conversation between their patient and his visitor and started talking between themselves in low voices.

"I think it's the only way to get you out of here," Linda continued. "That ridiculous hearing that your family set up wasn't your last chance. When I left the courtroom, I vowed to find some way to prevent them from railroading you into this horrible place. Alan and I think we can get you another hearing!"

"Alan?"

"Yes. You remember—Alan Quinn, my boss!"

Impassively, Mickey stood and stretched.

Linda watched and waited for several seconds; finally she couldn't stand it any longer. "Well, what do you think? You're a lawyer. Will it work?"

"Maybe," he said tonelessly, sitting closer to her than before.

"Then we have to try!" Impulsively, Linda threw her arms around Mickey's neck and kissed his cheek. "Oh, Mickey, I couldn't let them keep me away from you. I love you so much!"

With her hands clasped behind his neck and her head on his shoulder, Linda waited for his arms to encircle her. But nothing happened, except that Mickey started mumbling again. "Now I can get that cheating bastard. I'm going to slit his throat this time and laugh while he bleeds to death."

Linda froze. "W-what?" she asked, her eyes widening in horror.

Mickey grinned. "Once we get through this hearing process again, I'll be free. I can't carry out my plans until I'm free again. But when I am, he's mine—all mine."

"Who?" she whispered, her heart thundering. She glanced at the orderlies, but they were so wrapped up in their conversation that they hadn't heard a word.

"Bill!" Mickey rasped, then slid a cautious glance at the absorbed orderlies and lowered his voice. "Bill, that's who. He's the first person who's going to pay for his sins."

"Oh, no. Wait a minute. I think Bill has suffered enough," she said quickly, her throat dry. "You don't mean it. You're just a little confused. I think it's time to just take care of ourselves now."

"No way! No way has he paid for his sins! But he will," Mickey growled, his eyes gleaming. "When I get out, I'm going to track him down. And when I find him . . . this time he won't get away. I'm going to make him suffer before I kill him. The way he's made me suffer."

Linda shrank back from him in shock. For the first time she realized just how sick he really was. "Oh, God," she whispered, one hand clutching her throat. "Mickey, you've got to forget about the past. What's important now is the future. That's all you have now, and all you need. You can't change what's happened. You can only make plans for what's going to happen."

With a smirk, he said, "What's going to happen is that I'm going to slit Bill's throat."

"No!"

"Problems?" one of the orderlies asked. "Your time's about up."

"Just a few more minutes, please," Linda begged, trying to calm down. There was nothing to panic about, not really. She just had to convince Mickey to forget about the past.

"Okay, but wrap it up." The orderly turned back to his friend.

Linda, her palms sweating, pinned Mickey with her eyes. "You can't say or even think things like that, or you'll never get out of here!" She inched away from him.

"Laura?" he said.

"Laura. What about her?"

Mickey reached up and twirled a strand of Linda's blond hair around his finger. "Laura." Images out of the past raced in a crazy kaleidoscope through his mind.

"Mickey, please. You're scaring me!"

"Sorry." Mickey dropped his hand, rose and walked over to his closet. He could see her reflection in the mirror, see the worry in her blue eyes, the pale cast of her skin, just as if she'd been lying to him. But of course she had. Laura had always lied to him.

Reaching for the corner of the mirror, he pulled out the molding, and his carefully concealed weapon slipped neatly into his hands. Then he lunged.

Linda saw the hatred and maniacal fervor in his eyes. Before she could move, he was on her, some shiny object flashing in his right hand.

"You lied to me, Laura, and I'm going to kill you!"

"W-what? Oh, God!" Linda screamed.

Before the orderlies even knew what was happening, Mickey leapt at Linda and knocked her to the floor.

The slimmer orderly sprang on him. Mickey was strong, but between them, the orderlies were able to pull him away from Linda. She was screaming wildly as she scrambled up and backed toward the door.

As Mickey was wrestled to the ground, his crude weapon fell and smashed to pieces on the hard tile floor. At the sound of the glass shattering, he abruptly stopped struggling, just as the door flew open and Dr. Powell, his face white, ran into the room. "What's going on here?" he demanded.

The larger orderly was breathing hard. "He jumped her. With that." He pointed to the splintered glass on the floor. He and the slimmer man hoisted Mickey onto the bed.

"Get Ms. Phillips out of here!" the doctor ordered, then touched her shoulder. "Are you all right?"

Her eyes were wide and terrified, but she tried to pull herself together. "Y-yes, I'm fine," she whispered.

Dr. Powell turned to his patient. "Mickey?"

But Mickey Horton had withdrawn into his shell. He lay on his bed as if nothing had happened, though the orderlies were panting as they held his shoulders down.

"Clean this up," Dr. Powell ordered, waving at the mess on the floor as a nurse hurried into Mickey's room. "And make sure that the front desk knows that Mr. Horton is to have *no* visitors. Not even family members!"

"Yes, sir."

Turning back to his patient, the doctor waved the orderlies aside. "He's all right now."

"Linda? Is that you?" Mickey asked suddenly as she passed through the door and paused outside in the hallway. "What are you doing here?"

"She's leaving," Dr. Powell said sternly. He turned to Linda. "Please wait for me in the reception area."

"Okay," she whispered, still shaken and cold inside. She loved Mickey with all her heart and could hardly believe that he had attacked her. He'd hit her once before, on the night he'd caught her lying when she'd tried to convince him that Melissa was his daughter. But that was different. This . . . this attack had been maniacal. Suddenly she was reminded of another such attack, which she'd tried desperately to forget: on the night the Hortons claimed that Mickey had attacked Bill, he had also mistaken Linda for his ex-wife and tried to strangle her.

"Just have a seat," the nurse at the main desk said. Linda sat on the edge of her chair and waited. She picked up an old magazine and leafed through it, then lifted her eyes as the front door opened and Maggie Horton, her cheeks red from the wind, walked into the hospital. Her smile froze when she saw Linda.

"What're you doing here?" Maggie asked tightly.

"I, um, had some information for Mickey," Linda replied.

"You've seen him?"

"Yes."

Maggie didn't trust Linda. "I didn't think anyone but family was supposed to see my husband," she said, turning to the nurse at the desk.

"Dr. Powell okayed it," the nurse said, just as Dr. Powell himself strode into the reception area.

"Mrs. Horton!"

"Hi. I'd like to see Mickey."

"I'm afraid that's impossible right now. He's resting."

"But *she* just saw him!" Maggie saw Linda shift her eyes away. "And she's not even a family member."

"It was a legal matter," the doctor replied curtly.

"Fine. Just let me see Mickey."

"I can't. Not today." He glanced nervously at Linda. Her blond hair was wild, her cheeks still flaming.

"Why not?" Maggie persisted.

"Ms. Phillips's visit upset him a little."

"How?"

"I don't know. But I'll find out."

"I want to know all about it!" Maggie said, looking pointedly at Linda. "Mickey's *my* husband, and I don't want him upset!"

"I understand, Mrs. Horton. It won't happen again," Dr. Powell assured her.

"When can I see him?"

"Just let me see how he does for the rest

of the afternoon. Why don't you call tomorrow?"

"Tomorrow." Maggie didn't like being kept away from Mickey, but there wasn't a lot she could do about it. Dr. Powell had obviously made up his mind—because of Linda Phillips. She looked angrily at the blond woman. "I will. And here, let me leave you my new address and phone number, in case you want to reach me." She wrote the information down on a small slip of paper. "Let me know the minute I can see him."

"I will," Dr. Powell promised.

"And, Dr. Powell?"

"Yes?"

"I don't want this woman to see my husband again."

"Not even if I think it will help him?" he asked.

Maggie glared at Linda. "No."

"I'm only trying to help your husband," Dr. Powell said kindly.

Her shoulders slumped. "Okay. But please call me first," Maggie said. "I only want what's best for Mickey."

"Of course."

Linda avoided Maggie's eyes. So the wimpy farm girl had a backbone after all.

"Now, Ms. Phillips. If I can have a minute of your time . . ." Dr. Powell led Linda down a private corridor.

Maggie gazed after them, feeling like an outsider. *What's going on?* she wondered, a chill of dread sliding down her spine.

Linda could feel Maggie's eyes on her

back, but she didn't turn around. The little bumpkin could guess all she wanted. As far as what had happened in Mickey's room, Linda's lips were sealed. She wasn't going to tell anyone.

Dr. Powell shut the door of his office behind her. "Sit down," he said, indicating one of the chairs in front of his desk in the small, cluttered room. "Well? Can you tell me your version of what happened?"

Linda sat on the edge of her chair and shook her head. "I don't really know, doctor. He seemed fine. We were talking about the future, and then the next thing I knew, he was screaming 'You lied to me, Laura, and I'm going to kill you,' or something like that. Then . . . then he lunged at me." She shuddered, thinking of the deadly glass knife. "It was as if he didn't know me."

"Did you say something to trigger his outbreak?"

Linda thought about the conversation and decided to keep quiet about Mickey's threats against his brother. "No, we were just making some plans for when he gets out."

"And he wasn't upset?"

Linda shook her head. "Not then. He was looking forward to being free again."

"So, what changed things?"

"I don't know. He just snapped."

"Did he talk about his brother?"

Linda went cold inside. "I couldn't really hear. He . . . he mumbled a lot," she lied.

"But he mentioned Laura?"

"Yes."

Dr. Powell knew that he wasn't getting the whole story, but he had no way to prove it. Obviously, Linda Phillips wasn't going to be completely honest. "Considering what happened this afternoon," he said slowly, "I think that, for the time being, it's not a good idea for you to see Mickey. There's something about you that triggers these outbursts, and until we find out what it is, it's not safe for you—or him."

"But I have to see him!" she said, her voice rising.

"We can't risk it."

"You don't understand—"

"Yes, Ms. Phillips, I do. I didn't want to turn his wife away, and I don't want to restrict you. But I have to put your safety and Mickey's mental condition at the top of my list of priorities."

Linda was outraged. Maggie had done this to her! "How long is this going to last? Is this ultimatum just for me, or is it going to apply to all visitors?"

"You heard what I said to his wife."

"But she doesn't care about him!"

The doctor's eyebrows twitched upward. "Is that so?" He studied Linda with interested eyes.

"Well, maybe a little. But I really do care for him, Dr. Powell. I just want him to be happy!"

"Then stay away—at least for a while. I need a couple days to work with him alone before anyone else sees him. Of course, the immediate family can insist, but I hope they'll see my point of view. If you'd like, I could give you a call when he is able to see you."

"I'd appreciate it," she said stiffly, and stood.

"Thank you."

Linda made her way out of the hospital. She frowned when she recognized Maggie's truck, still parked in the lot. *So the farm girl hasn't given up,* she thought as she climbed into her car. *Well, neither have I!*

Chapter Three
New Beginnings

Laura Horton glanced at Bill as he parked the car in the lot at Brookville Hospital. "I want to bring him home," she repeated. "I want us all to be a family. You, me, Michael and Jennifer Rose."

"I know you do, sweetheart, but Dr. Chamberlain wants to keep an eye on Michael for a while longer." He offered her a crooked smile that softened the lines of his face and touched his sky-blue eyes.

"We're both doctors. We could take care of him," she insisted.

Bill sighed and raked his fingers through his hair. "You're still recuperating from a difficult birth, Jennifer is barely a week old, and I'm having a lot of trouble with my arm."

"It seems so long ago that Mickey shot you," Laura whispered.

Bill's face was grim as he thought about the hatred in his brother's eyes that night.

"That part's over. But we can't really take care of Michael at home."

"Your mother could stop by if we needed help."

"No, she's still busy with Hope, and she will be until Doug gets back from Chicago. God only knows when that'll be." He placed a comforting hand on her arm when he saw the tears gathering in her eyes. "Do you think I don't want him back with us? Don't you know that I'm dying to tell him that he's really my son? After all these years, I can't wait to tell him the truth."

"But you won't, will you?" she asked urgently. "Not until he's strong enough to handle it."

"Scout's honor," he promised. "Just remember that when he comes home someone might let it out; he could get hold of an old newspaper telling about the hearing. I don't want him to find out that way, Laura. I want to be the one to tell him."

Laura looked into his serious eyes and kissed his cheek. "I love you," she whispered.

"And I love you." He wrapped his arms around her and held her close, whispering into her golden hair. "And as soon as possible, we'll all be a family. I promise. Now, come on. Let's not keep him waiting."

Together they walked through the main doors of the hospital and hurried to Michael's room. He was lying in bed, staring at the ceiling, his sheets crumpled around him. He turned as they came into the room, and a boyish smile sliced across his face when he saw his mother.

" 'Bout time you showed up," he said, teasing. "Where's the baby?"

"Julie's watching her for a little while." Laura squeezed his hands. "How're you feeling, hmm? Are they treating you well?"

"Okay, I guess. But I want to get out of here."

"You will, you will, just as soon as Dr. Chamberlain releases you. I've got your old room ready and—"

"Whoa, Mom." He glanced at Bill, then back to his mother. "I was hoping to move back with Trish. If she still wants me."

"Oh, Michael, you can't—"

"Shh." Bill's fingers tightened on Laura's shoulders. "We'll talk about this later," he said, looking at his son. Michael had never trusted him; worse, he still believed that Mickey was his father, and it hurt Bill not to be able to tell him the truth. Wincing inwardly, he walked over to the window and leaned against the ledge. "The first thing we have to do is get you well."

"I'm feeling fine."

"Are you?" Bill glanced at the chart hanging on the end of Michael's bed, and the lines around his mouth eased. "I guess you are. It shouldn't be long before Dr. Chamberlain springs you."

"Thank God!" Michael said, leaning back on the pillows and avoiding his mother's anxious eyes. "So tell me—how's Jennifer?"

"Couldn't be better," Laura answered.

Michael felt a tiny stab of jealousy. Now Mom had a child with Bill; she didn't need him anymore. And the fact that Bill was here was a reminder to Michael that the new baby was really just his half sister. "You know, this place is starting to drive me nuts," he grumbled.

Bill chuckled and winked at his wife. "From my experience, I'd say you're getting well. The grumpier the patient gets, the healthier he is."

"Is that right, *doctor?*" Michael couldn't hide the sarcasm in his voice. Bill had always gotten under his skin. "So why won't they let me see a newspaper? I can't even read the sports page!"

Bill's smile faded. "I'll try to do something about that."

"Good. Now, tell me all about the baby."

"Jennifer's doing just fine," Laura assured him. "We had her checked out at the hospital as a precaution because she was slightly premature. But everything is perfectly normal. And, personally, I think she's the most beautiful little girl in the world."

"But your mother might be a tad prejudiced," Bill added.

"I am not! The nurses in pediatrics think she's beautiful, and so do you!"

"I can't argue with that."

"So, uh, how's Dad doing? When can I see him?" Michael asked, studying Laura's face. Was it his imagination or did she blanch?

"He's still recovering, Mike," she said, glancing nervously at Bill.

"Recovering? What's that supposed to mean, recovering?"

"I told you the other day that this—your accident and his regaining some of his memory and all—has been very hard on your—on Mickey. He's been going through a lot, trying to remember his past."

"And my accident made it worse?" Michael felt a pang of guilt.

"No! Uh, we don't know exactly what's happened. But he's being tested by psychiatrists."

"Why can't you handle it? You're a psychiatrist!"

"He has another doctor," Laura said, wondering how to end this no-win conversation. She didn't want to lie to Michael, not anymore, but she had to protect him. "It's going to be a little while before he completely comes to grips with all that has happened to him since the amnesia."

Michael eyed her suspiciously. "There's nothing wrong with him, is there? I feel like nobody's giving me any straight answers. Even Maggie won't talk about him. I ask questions and she just clams up. I thought she liked me."

"She does," Laura said quickly. "She cares about you very much. But she's got the farm to worry about, as well as Mickey's memory and his past. It's a lot for her to handle."

Michael pulled on his lower lip. His mother was nervous about something—something to do with Mickey. And the way she kept glancing at Bill for support wasn't right. Something was going on. "How come I can't see him? Why can't I give him a call and talk to him?"

"Because you're still recuperating," Bill said, placing his hand on Michael's shoulder. The boy cringed away from his touch. Bill dropped his hand and gritted his teeth to keep from blurting out the truth. The entire family had agreed to keep the secret from Michael until he was strong enough to handle it. "Mickey isn't really seeing anyone just yet. He's working with a counselor and trying to put his life back into some semblance of order. He really doesn't want to see any of the family until he does that."

"Can't you help him?" Michael asked his mother.

"Not until he asks for it."

"We're all willing to do anything we can to help him," Bill said. "But we have to be patient." He tried to put his arm around Laura, but pain from the bullet wound seared up his arm and he paled, grimacing and remembering that horrible night all over again.

Michael's eyes widened. "Bill? What's wrong? You okay?"

Bill forced a grin. "Oh, yeah. No problem. You remember, I twisted my arm the night of Jennifer's birth. That was quite an ordeal trudging through the snow and all."

Michael pretended to listen as his mother and Bill talked again about the night Jennifer was born, but he didn't really care. His thoughts had settled on his father and the fact that everyone in his family acted strangely whenever he asked about Mickey.

Something was wrong—very wrong. As soon as he was on his feet, he was going to find out what it was.

When Bill and Laura finally left, Michael slid out of bed and peeked down the hall toward the nurses' station. He was in luck—they were all busy and didn't notice him.

Grimacing as he felt his stitches pull a bit, he slipped on his robe and sneaked down the hallway toward the waiting room, where last week's newspapers were probably scattered. He planned to grab a couple, hurry back to his room and catch up on the sports—and whatever other news there was in Salem. Maybe the papers would give him an inkling of what was happening with his dad.

Then he stopped dead in his tracks as a thought knifed through his mind. *What if Dad is dead?* His heart began to pound with fear. There had to be a reason he wasn't allowed to see a newspaper. Maybe everyone was hiding the fact that Mickey had been killed while trying to save him!

He inched down the hall to the empty waiting room and picked up the first newspapers he found. Sweat dotting his brow, he tucked the crumpled pages inside his robe and started back to his room.

"Mr. Horton!" a stern voice said.

Michael nearly jumped out of his skin.

"What're you doing out of bed?" said Nurse Stevens, pursing her lips and clucking her tongue.

Michael froze. "I, er, was just stretching my legs," he offered lamely.

"Well, you get right back to your room and into bed, and stay there until Dr. Chamberlain says it's okay for you to go strolling around the halls. Dinner's almost ready. Go on. Scoot!"

"I will," Michael said, praying that the papers wouldn't drop to the floor. "I can hardly wait to eat."

The nurse eyed him skeptically. "You're the first patient who has ever said that."

"I . . . I'm used to eating cafeteria food," he said. "My mom and her husband are both doctors."

"Sure." Nurse Stevens guided him back to his room. "Let me help you into bed."

"No! Uh, first I need to use the restroom," he said.

"Okay. You call me if you need me."

"I will. Promise." He slipped into the small bath and closed the door behind him, just as the newspapers slid to the floor. Breathing a sigh of relief, he waited for a few minutes, glancing at the headlines on the sports page, and then, when the coast was clear, sneaked back into his bed. "Okay. Let's just see what's been happening in Salem!" he murmured to himself as he scanned the front page of a paper from over a week ago. It was dated a couple days after his accident. "Perfect!"

Doug opened one eye and reached for the phone. He punched out the number for the airport from memory and was surprised when he was connected.

"May I help you?" a cheery voice asked.

Pushing himself upright, he explained that he wanted to get back to Salem.

"I think I can arrange that."

Hallelujah! "Great!" he exclaimed.

He was given the number of an airline flying to Salem, and upon calling the ticket counter, was assured that his old ticket would be honored. He could be back in Salem by late afternoon!

He showered, shaved, dressed and packed in record time. Whistling as he cinched his tie around his neck, he glanced out the window and noticed blue sky above the skyline of Chicago. Things were definitely looking up, he thought as he headed out the door to grab a bite to eat.

He took the elevator to the first floor and, on entering the coffee shop, spotted Kim drinking a cup of coffee and reading the paper.

She glanced up and smiled when she saw him. "Good morning. You look like a million bucks today."

"That's because I feel like a million bucks. How about you?"

She took another sip of coffee. "I'm as good as I can be—under the circumstances. I'm going to miss you, though."

"Miss me?"

"Yes. I'm not going back to Salem with you. Sorry, Doug, but you're going to have to work things out with Julie on your own."

Doug sighed, sat down across from her and ordered toast and coffee.

Fumbling in her purse, Kim found a cigarette and lit up, her fingers shaking. "I guess I have to think things through. For the last couple of years I've had my hopes pinned on you, and now . . ." She lifted a shoulder and sipped her coffee. "Time for Plan B."

"Which is?"

"I wish I knew," she whispered, then cleared her throat. "But I'll come up with it. Soon."

The waitress put Doug's breakfast in front of him. When she had gone, he tested his coffee, watching Kim. "I'd like you to explain to Julie why you lied."

She shook her head.

"All right, I won't force you." Doug felt himself softening toward her. "You should head home."

"Home?" Kim smiled humorlessly. "Where's that? I haven't really lived anywhere since I lost you. It seems I've just been the stranger in town everywhere I've gone these past few years while I've been looking for you."

"Look, I'm sorry—"

She waved away his apology and fought a losing battle with tears.

"Now, don't go getting maudlin on me, Kim. Pull yourself together and get on with your life. You're still young and attractive—you can do anything you want."

Kim blinked back her tears and tossed her hair over her shoulder. "Maybe you're right. But I would like to go to the airport with you."

Doug still didn't really trust her, but her

dark eyes seemed so wistful that he couldn't say no. "Okay," he said slowly, finishing his coffee. "I'll meet you back down in the lobby in an hour."

"Thanks."

She rose to go up to her room, wishing that there were some way of hanging onto him. But it was useless. He loved Julie, and that was that.

An hour later she was seated beside him in a cab. She couldn't say a word. She stayed by Doug's side as he stood in line, exchanged his tickets and put his baggage through. Her face was sorrowful, though she refused to break down.

Finally, all the arrangements were made, and he seemed to notice the sadness in her face for the first time. "Maybe this wasn't such a good idea, your coming out here. You seem pretty down. Why don't you just take off now? You don't need to wait for the plane to leave," he said.

"I'm fine. Really."

"Good." He gave her a smile that nearly broke her heart. "Look, the plane might be delayed here for a while. There's really no reason for you to sit out here and get bored. Go back to the hotel," he suggested. "Work out Plan B. Okay?"

"Maybe you're right," she whispered. "But before I go, Doug, there's something I have to tell you."

Here it comes, Doug thought, bracing himself.

"I really want nothing but the best for you.

I wish you all the happiness in the world with Julie, and I hope everything works out the way you want it to." She swallowed hard, fighting her emotions.

"Thanks, Kim."

"Wait, there's something else. I think I should warn you."

"About what?"

"I . . . I have this feeling deep down inside that it's not over. Someday—I don't know when or for how long—but someday, you're going to be mine again."

"Oh, Kim, you're wrong. It's over."

She reached up and clasped her arms about his neck. Pressing her lips to his, she kissed him hungrily. Then, just as suddenly as she had embraced him, she pulled away. She spun on her heel and ran down the concourse and out of Doug Williams's life.

"Why are you all dolled up—going somewhere special?" David asked as his mother stepped into his room. She was wearing a cream-colored skirt and sweater, and her dark hair was swept onto her head.

She smiled at his backhanded compliment and picked up a pair of his jeans that were on the floor near his bed. Since his return from the hospital, he had used his "weakened condition" to his advantage. His room was a disaster. "What's this, the third degree?"

"No, but I thought that Doug was still out of town. When did he get back?"

Julie blanched, then recovered. She'd sworn to get Doug Williams out of her mind.

actually looking forward to seeing him again. She'd always had a soft spot in her heart for the easygoing attorney.

Don, grinning from ear to ear, was waiting for her at a corner table. A candle threw its flickering light against the walls and a single red rose bloomed in the vase in front of the empty chair.

"Oh, Don," Julie whispered, lifting the flower and smelling its sweet fragrance. "It's beautiful."

"So are you."

"I'm not late, am I?" she asked as he held out her chair.

"No, no, you're right on time. I would have picked you up, but—"

"No apologies. Okay? I know you've been busy."

He grinned. "Everyone and his dog wants to sue Syntron for that explosion."

"Good business for you."

"Maybe. Depends upon what caused the fire." The waiter appeared and Don ordered a carafe of wine. "But let's not talk about work. I've had enough of that for one day."

Julie's blue eyes twinkled. "All right, counselor," she agreed as he poured them each a glass of Chablis. She lifted her glass and touched it to his. "No shoptalk."

He leaned back in his chair and looked at her. "You really do look great," he said.

Blushing slightly, Julie showed the hint of a dimple. "Thanks."

"I'm only telling you the truth. You're the most beautiful woman I've ever seen." Then, feeling awkward, he cleared his throat.

Sipping her wine, Julie glanced around the dimly lit room. Wicker baskets hung above the heavy wooden tables. Exposed pipes and beams overhead ran across the ceiling, and a lone violinist roamed slowly between the tables, giving the place an old European flavor. "Why did you pick this restaurant?"

"Have you ever been here before?"

Julie shook her head. "No, never."

"Good. I didn't think so. It's relatively new, and it has two things going for it."

"What do you mean?"

"First, a talisman is like a magic figure—a good-luck charm. I thought I might need some good luck. For us."

"Oh."

"Second, it isn't haunted for you by old memories of Doug."

Doug again. Her heart twisted painfully and her teeth sank into her lower lip. If only she could quit thinking about him. "I'd rather not talk about him," she said softly, her throat dry.

"My mistake."

"Don't worry about it."

"Maybe we should dance a little."

"Maybe."

"Or, better yet, just talk about us," he suggested.

Her smile trembled. "Okay." Lifting her glass to his, Julie looked into Don's compassionate brown eyes. "To . . . tonight!"

"Tonight and always." He clinked his glass with hers, and knew that he was falling hopelessly in love with her all over again.

Chapter Four

Confusion

•

"The captain has turned on the No Smoking sign and it's time to fasten your seat belts as we begin our final descent. . . ."

Doug stretched and looked out the small window at the winking lights of Salem far below. He was home at last!

Get ready, Julie. I'm coming to get you, he thought as the plane touched down and taxied to a stop. He reached for his bag in the overhead compartment and couldn't get off the plane fast enough.

Picking up his suitcase from the baggage claim, he headed for the parking lot and climbed into his car. The engine of his Triumph sputtered against the cold but finally caught. He slammed the little car into gear and roared to the gate, paid his fee and then headed down the freeway. Toward Julie.

His heart soared when he saw lights blazing in her front window. Without a second thought, he parked in the drive and bounded up the steps to ring the bell.

When no one answered, he rang again, more impatiently. "Julie?" he called.

The door opened a crack and David, his head wrapped in a bandage, peered out. At the sight of Doug, David frowned.

"Hi, is your mom home?" Doug asked.

"She's out," David said.

"Where?"

"Some new restaurant, I think. I don't really know."

"What happened to you?" Doug asked.

David shrugged. He'd never cared much for Doug and had only put up with him because his mom had been so head-over-heels in love with the guy. "I was down on the docks during the Syntron Chemical plant explosion." When he saw the concern in Doug's eyes, David looked away. "I'm okay, though. I'll tell Mom you stopped by."

"Wait a minute—don't you remember the name of that restaurant?"

David thought for a moment. Julie had left less than an hour before. Maybe he should tell Doug; let him find out that Julie wasn't pining away for him. "I . . . I really can't remember," he lied, not knowing what to do.

"I really need to talk to her."

"I'll let her know."

Doug wasn't easily fooled. "Who's she with?" he asked slowly, eyeing the boy.

"A friend."

"*Which* friend?"

"Beats me. She didn't really say. Just that

she'd be home around midnight or so. I'll tell her you came by."

"I'd appreciate it."

The door shut, and Doug was left standing on the porch. He checked his watch. It was barely eight o'clock. Julie was out? Where? And with whom? The same sense of dread he'd felt in Chicago crept up his spine. What the hell was going on?

Climbing back into his car, Doug drove over to check on his nightclub, Doug's Place. Then he headed for Tom and Alice Horton's house, where his daughter had been staying.

"Daddy!" the little girl exclaimed, hopping off her chair and running up to him when he opened the kitchen door. The smell of cinnamon and freshly baked bread filled the room, and he smiled. It was good to be home. He'd always thought of the Horton house as home, even after his wife, Addie, had passed away. Addie's mother, Alice, had been more of a mother to him than his own mother ever had.

"Hi, princess!" Doug scooped Hope off her feet and twirled her in the air. Her chubby arms wrapped around his neck, and she squealed in delight. "Miss me?"

"Bunches and bunches!"

"Me, too," he whispered, looking over the tousled black curls at Alice.

"Good to see you, Doug," she said. "We were worried about you, stranded in Chicago all this time."

He saw the lines of strain around her mouth. "I read about the explosion on the docks. University Hospital must have been a madhouse."

"It was." Then she glanced at Hope. "But this little girl was an absolute dream, weren't you?"

"You bet!" Hope said, squirming from Doug's arms down to the ground and running up the stairs to find her doll.

Doug leaned against the counter and took the cup of tea that Alice offered.

"How about some banana bread or a cinnamon roll?" Alice asked.

"No, thanks. This'll do. Has Julie been by to see Hope?" he asked.

Alice shook her head. "No, but she's been busy. We all have. Julie helped out at the hospital during the explosion, and then there was the hearing. . . ." Her voice trailed off, and pain clouded her eyes.

"I read a little about it."

"It's rather complicated. Tom and I don't exactly see eye to eye on what happened. We've all been pretty wrapped up with Mickey, I'm afraid, not really sure if what we're doing is right."

"I stopped by Julie's house. David said she was out."

Alice's brows rose. "First I've heard of it."

"Then you don't know where she is?"

"No, but, believe me, she deserves a night out. She worked till she dropped at the hospital, and since then she's been taking care of David and Jennifer Rose."

"Jennifer who?"

Alice's eyes lighted up. "Oh, obviously you

don't know about the latest addition to the Horton clan. Well, come into the living room, and I'll show you the pictures."

Doug followed her and sat on the couch as she filled him in on what had happened. She showed him the first snapshots of Bill and Laura's daughter.

"Sounds like I missed a lot while I was gone."

Dragging her doll by one foot, Hope bounded down the stairs. "Where's Kim?" she asked innocently.

Doug's brow furrowed. "She's still in Chicago."

"Isn't she coming home?"

"No, honey, Salem isn't really her home."

"But I like her!" Hope said, thrusting out her lower lip.

"I know."

Alice shook her head. "That's all she talked about while you were gone," she said. "She seems to think that Kim's going to be her new mother."

"What!" Doug was stunned.

"It's true, isn't it?" Hope demanded.

"No, honey," Doug said gently. "Julie's going to be your new mommy. Remember?"

"Don't like Julie!" Hope crossed her arms firmly over her chest.

Alice's lips compressed into a thin line. "It's been this way for the past couple days," she admitted. "I'm afraid that somehow Hope's got the notion that you were going to marry Kim."

"Please, Daddy."

Doug was angry with Kim all over again.

Though she'd been good to Hope, Kim had obviously made promises to the little girl that were completely out of line. "Honey, I'm going to marry Julie." He glanced up at Alice. "And I think I'd better get that straightened out right away."

"I want Kim!"

"Look, princess, get your coat and bags and we'll go home tonight and talk about it."

Hope looked worriedly at her grandmother. "Not tonight!"

"I'm afraid this is my fault," Alice murmured. "We didn't know when you were getting into town, so Tom and I promised to take her ice-skating tomorrow morning."

"And the restaurant," Hope reminded her.

"Right. That new restaurant, Talismans. Tomorrow night with Grandpa."

"New restaurant?" Doug asked.

"Yes. It just opened last week—somewhere on the riverfront. As a matter of fact, we heard about it from Julie."

"Julie?"

"Mm-hm. She mentioned to Tom that she was going there some night this week."

Doug's eyes flashed. "When?"

"She didn't say."

"Can't I please stay, Daddy?" Hope asked, tugging on his jacket.

"It's all right with us," Alice assured him.

Doug bent on one knee and brushed Hope's hair out of her eyes. "If you promise to be good."

"I will!"

"Okay." He hugged her, and then she pattered back up the stairs. "I'll check in with you tomorrow," he said. "But right now, I'd better find Julie and straighten things out with her."

When he left the Horton house, he felt uneasy. Things weren't right. He could feel it. He'd left Salem after a huge fight with Julie, and then he'd been trapped in Chicago, unable to get through to her.

His jaw clenched and his fingers tightened around the wheel as he squinted against the oncoming headlights and drove toward the riverfront—toward Talismans.

After pouring the last drops from the bottle of wine into Julie's glass, Don stared into her blue eyes and wished to God that he didn't love her. She'd hurt him once before, yet here he was again, in the same spot.

He touched his glass to hers. "I've had a terrific time, Julie. Thanks for coming out with me. Here's to . . ."

"Us?" she whispered, blushing slightly.

"Us," he agreed.

Julie's throat constricted. Don had been so good to her, while Doug had given her nothing but heartache. At the thought of Doug, she died a little inside. She loved him so much—too much—and she had to forget him. "I've had a terrific time, too, Don. But don't thank me for seeing you. I really enjoyed myself—just like I did last night at the pizza parlor and the night before at the movies." She took a sip of wine. "You've been wonderful."

"Only because I care for you."

Tears gathered in her eyes. "Thanks."

"Do you want me to give you a ride home?"

"I'd love it, but it doesn't make much sense, does it? We've each got our own cars."

He glanced at the empty bottle of wine.

Seeing the worry in his eyes, she touched his hand. "I'll be fine. Really. I'll just take it nice and easy." Then she looked up, and froze.

Doug was standing in the doorway of the restaurant, his blue eyes blazing as they bored into her. "Oh, God," she whispered, her face draining of color.

"Hey, are you all right?" Don asked, and then, following her gaze, lifted his eyes to see Doug Williams, his old nemesis, glaring at them as he wended his way through the tables. He stopped beside Julie's chair.

"I have to talk to you," Doug whispered to Julie, his eyes glued to her face.

"I don't think this is the time—"

"I've been trying to get hold of you for days," he said, "but I just found out the phones were out. With all that's happened here in Salem, I've been worried sick about you."

Julie wouldn't believe him. He'd lied to her too often before. "I've been just fine. Now, if you'll excuse us—" She started to get up to leave, but he grabbed her wrist.

"I need to talk to you."

"Later, Doug."

His eyes narrowed. "I don't understand."

"Don't you?" she repeated, her voice low. "Well, why don't you tell me how Kim is? She was in Chicago with you, wasn't she?"

"But I went to Chicago to find out about the divorce."

"Sure. And Kim just tagged along."

"Yes!" Doug sighed, trying to keep hold of his temper. "The important thing is what I found in Chicago."

"Not another ex-wife, I hope!" Julie said, cringing at the bitter sound of her own words. As she gazed into Doug's furious eyes, she knew that she still loved him, but her pride was on the line.

"Just listen to me. I'm free! The divorce was final all along. Don't you see? Now we can get married."

She felt as if he'd slapped her. Get married? *Now?* After all the pain she'd suffered? "I don't think we should be discussing this."

"Then let's just leave. We can find a justice of the peace and get married by morning."

"You can't be serious!" she gasped.

"I've never been more serious in my life." He held her with his eyes, and she wanted to believe him—just trust him once more.

Don eyed the two of them and felt a fresh flood of anger engulf him. "Maybe I'd better go."

"No." Julie's gaze shifted to him. "This is our night," she said, her voice catching as she struggled with her conflicting emotions.

Doug was shocked; his eyes narrowed dangerously as they swung to Don. "Wait a minute! You mean that since I've been gone, you and Don. . . "

"Have become very close," Julie said proudly.

"But that's crazy! You and I have plans!"

"And you changed them. You and Kim."

"Kim has nothing to do with this!"

Her eyes grew cold. "You don't know how much I'd like to believe that. But I can't."

"Why not?" Doug demanded, his voice low.

Don had seen enough. He stood, and met Doug's eyes. "I think the lady is politely asking you to leave her alone. Why don't you just take the hint?"

"Stay out of it, Craig," Doug warned.

"I can't."

"This is between Julie and me."

"And me," Don insisted. "Come on, Julie, let's get out of here. You can leave your car. I'll take you home."

Doug's anger flared. His hands clenched and relaxed and clenched again, and he stood poised on the balls of his feet, his eyes trained on the calm gaze of the attorney. He wanted to drive his fist right into Don's pompous face.

"Don't even think about it, Williams," Don muttered, his chin thrust forward, an easy target. "Because you're going to be biting off one helluva lot more than you can chew. I've had my fill of you and the way you've treated Julie. If you make the first move, I guarantee it'll be your last."

"Is there a problem here?" the maître d'

asked anxiously as he walked briskly to the table.

"Nothing we can't handle," Doug said. Seeing the fury in the set of Don's jaw, and realizing the futility of a confrontation right now, he backed down. Glancing at Julie one last time, he said, "I'll call you in the morning." Then he turned on his heel and strode out of the restaurant.

Julie looked anxiously at Don. "I . . . I didn't mean for you to get involved in all that," she said.

"It would've happened sometime."

She blinked back her tears. "I just don't want you to think that I'm using you," she whispered.

Wrapping his arm around her shoulders, he stared deep into her eyes. "I don't know what bothers me more, Julie—the thought that you'll use me again . . . or the thought that you won't."

"Never," she whispered, looking at the door and silently praying that she'd find a way to forget Doug forever.

The new apartment had required a great deal of cleaning and scrubbing, but Maggie was finally starting to see progress. Grabbing a cola from the small refrigerator, she sank onto the old, claw-footed sofa and relaxed for the first time in days. Between running to Brookville to see Michael, waiting around Bayview to find out about Mickey, and driving back and forth from the farm, she was exhausted.

Then she noticed the time and realized she

was already late. "Wonderful," she muttered, finishing her drink before changing into clean slacks and a sweater. "Always a day late and a dollar short."

Grabbing her purse and jacket, she locked the door behind her and set out for Brookville. Visiting hours were almost over by the time she reached the hospital.

She hurried through the lobby and nearly ran into Dr. Chamberlain as she rounded the final corner on the way to Michael's room.

"You'd better slow down, Mrs. Horton," he advised, offering her a kind smile.

"I guess you're right. I was just in a hurry to see Michael."

"He's been asking about you."

"Yeah, I'm late. He told me that he might be released by the the end of the week. Is that true?"

"If things continue as they are, I see no reason why he can't go home and recuperate there. We'll know for sure in another day or two."

"Wonderful!"

Dr. Chamberlain continued down the hall, and Maggie knocked softly on Michael's door. She poked her head in. "Need some company?" she asked.

Michael was sitting up in bed and reading a magazine. He looked up as she came into the room. "Sure."

"Gee, honey, you look a whole lot better. How're you feeling?"

"Not too bad," he said, his eyes searching hers. "I was starting to think maybe you weren't coming."

"I said I would, didn't I? Look, I'm sorry for being late. I was cleaning up and just sat down to rest for a minute. The next thing I knew, it was past dinnertime. But, here I am, and I brought these." She reached into her pocket and pulled out a bag of licorice jelly beans.

"You didn't!"

"Just don't tell your mother, okay? She'd probably kill me."

"I don't think so."

Maggie winked at him. "This'll just be our little secret. Right?" she said, laughing.

Michael nodded and set the jelly beans aside. His fingers twisted the sheet beside him, and he looked away from her. "How's Dad?"

"I don't know what to say. No better, no worse. It's just going to take time, from everything I've been told." Maggie said, hating to evade the boy's questions.

"He still doesn't want to come and see me?"

Maggie could see the pain in his eyes. "Is that what you think?"

"I don't know what to think. No one seems to want to tell me the truth."

"Well, you know that your father loves you very much."

"Do I?"

"Sure, you don't have to worry about that. I think he needs your help as much as you need his. He needs you to be strong enough to give him the time to work things out on his own."

"With those psychiatrists, right?"

"Yes."

Michael's gaze shifted from the bed to her eyes. "Can't I call him, then, and talk to him?"

Frustrated, Maggie wished she could tell him everything. But she couldn't, not yet. She'd promised everyone, especially Michael's mother. So, gathering her strength, she continued the charade. "Your father blames himself for your accident—"

"But that's ridiculous!"

"We both know that, but it doesn't change things. He's carrying the blame for your accident around with him."

"Is that all?"

"No. When his memory returned, he had to sort out a whole lot of things from his past, such as your mother, his job, his parents. He needs more time to figure out where he belongs and what he wants to do. I don't think you should pressure him right now. Wait."

"You wouldn't lie to me, would you?" Michael asked softly.

"Of course not," she whispered, pushing his hair away from his face and hating herself. "Why? Do you think I would?"

"No. But everyone's been acting strange."

"It's hard on all of us. And we have to try to do what's best for you and Mickey."

"Is that what Mom and Bill told you?"

Surprised, Maggie nodded. "And your grandfather."

"Him, too?" Michael's shoulders drooped.

"We all love you, hon. We just want you to get well."

A nurse stepped into the room. "I'm sorry, Mrs. Horton, but visiting hours are over," she said quietly.

Maggie sighed and squeezed Michael's hand. "Next time I won't be late," she promised, rising and walking to the door.

"Don't worry about it." Michael waved to her and watched as she left. Then, once he was alone, he got out of bed and reached into his closet for the newspaper he'd found just two days ago in the reception area. He looked again at the picture of Mickey on the front page and the huge black headline that screamed at him: MICKEY HORTON FOUND INSANE; SALEM ATTORNEY COMMITTED TO BAYVIEW SANITARIUM.

Michael wadded up the paper and threw it back into the closet. What had happened to his dad, and why was everyone in his family lying to him?

Mickey sat upright on his bed with his head tilted back against the wall. Staring into the mirror he knew to be an observation window, he tried to melt the glass with his searing gaze.

He smiled as he thought back to his performance with Linda Phillips a few days before. *Pretty soon, they won't know if I'm coming or going,* he thought, laughing to himself.

A sudden knock on his door broke his train of thought. He swung his legs to the floor and waited as Dr. Powell walked into the room.

"Care to talk for a few minutes, Mickey?"

"Why not?" During the past few days, Dr. Powell had instigated several therapy sessions with Mickey and gotten nowhere. Another little professional chat wouldn't hurt. "Sounds like fun," Mickey added with a grin.

Pulling the chair up alongside the bed, Dr. Powell sat down and took a pen from his coat pocket. "You don't mind if I take a few notes while we talk, do you?"

"Not at all. I'm used to it. Did the same thing as a lawyer." Mickey winked and nodded. "Go ahead, take good notes."

The doctor grimaced. Sometimes he felt as if Mickey was baiting him. "Would you like to go back and practice law? Have you given that any thought?"

"I've given everything lots of thought these last few days, Doc."

"Care to elaborate on that?"

"What do you want to know?"

"How do you feel about your brother?"

"Which one?"

"Bill." Dr. Powell's lips thinned.

Mickey's smile relaxed. "I'm really sorry that I lost control the other night."

"You're talking about the night that you shot him?"

"Right. I'm just glad I didn't do him any more harm than I did."

Dr. Powell stared into his shuttered eyes, searching for some clue to what Mickey was really feeling. "What about your father, and your former wife?"

"Laura." Mickey's gaze clouded for a second.

"Yes, Laura."

"Well, I guess that Laura, Bill and Dad were all just doing what they thought was best for me," he said without emotion. "There really isn't any way they can understand what it's like to not know who you are one minute, and remember *everything* the next. And I resented them for lying to me for so many years."

"Go on."

"I lost control for a while," Mickey admitted, stifling the urge to laugh out loud as the doctor scribbled in his note pad. "And who's to say that I won't again, for that matter? But I'm feeling stronger all the time."

"What happened the other day with Linda Phillips?"

"That's what I meant about losing control. We were just sitting around talking, and I was overcome with this paranoia that she was going to hurt me."

"So you lashed out at her?"

"I thought of it as self-defense."

"And the piece of glass?"

"I knocked against the mirror, and a piece broke off. I just grabbed it and went for her."

"Was there anything in particular that she said that triggered your fear?" Dr. Powell asked slowly, still observing his patient.

"Not that I remember. She was trying to explain to me about the possibility of another hearing to get me out of here. I was telling her that I might just as well stay here until everyone is sure I'm okay. Which reminds me—I think Laura should be my therapist."

"Laura?" Dr. Powell repeated incredulously. "Your ex-wife?"

"Yes."

The doctor weighed Mickey's suggestion, but he didn't like it. "Why Laura?"

Mickey rubbed his chin. "I think it would give us a chance to clear the air between us. She knows me and who I was . . . she understands some of my motivations better than anyone else would. And I think we could communicate very effectively. I respect her as a professional, and I just think it makes a lot of sense."

Dr. Powell remembered the phrase that Linda had told him Mickey screamed out: *You lied to me, Laura, and I'm going to kill you.* "Is there any other reason you'd like to have Laura handle your therapy sessions?"

Mickey frowned. "I have to figure out who I really am. It might help to start with my wife—er, ex-wife."

Dr. Powell wasn't so sure. "Do you think that the two of you can sit down and calmly discuss the events of the past without becoming upset?"

"I think so. Like I said, I feel stronger all the time. Since Linda left, I've had this feeling that I'm on the way now. Kind of like there was one last dam I had built with all this anger stored up behind it. When it finally broke, no more anger." He smiled crookedly and shrugged.

"That might be. But then again, there might be more dams downriver that we haven't come to yet. What do you think?"

"I suppose you're right, Doc. I might be

really messed up, like you say."

"I didn't say you were really messed up, Mickey. I think that therapy with a trained professional will help. But, as for it being Laura . . . well, I'll have to think about that."

Mickey had to bite his lip to keep it from curling into a sneer. So Powell hadn't fallen for his act—at least, not yet. "Do. Think about it."

Rising from his chair, Dr. Powell slipped his pen back into his pocket and closed his notebook. "I think it's getting late. You'd better turn in and get some rest. We'll see how you feel in the morning."

"Whatever you say, Doc. I'll be here."

When the dead bolts had slid into place, Mickey turned off the light and stretched out on his bed. He wasn't ready to go to sleep, though. There were still plans to be made. He knew that he had to make all the right moves if he was going to succeed.

Sooner or later I'm going to make him give me Laura. She's the key. Once I have her, everything else will fall into place. A smile crossed his lips as he closed his eyes and drifted off.

Chapter Five

Second Thoughts

Bill squinted against the glare of the morning sun as he drove toward Bayview. "So much for an early start," he muttered, cursing his luck as he inched around a curve. The drive was taking much longer than he had planned, and his stomach was in knots.

No one knew he'd planned to see Mickey, not even Laura. His conscience pricked a little, but he clamped his fingers around the wheel and stepped on the accelerator. He had to settle some things with Mickey, and he had to settle them alone.

When he reached Bayview, Bill talked Dr. Powell into letting him see Mickey, then waited until two orderlies accompanied him to Mickey's room. The hospital seemed stark and sterile, and the sound of the dead bolts sliding back as an orderly unlocked the door made Bill's skin crawl. His own brother, institutionalized.

The door swung open, and Bill saw his

brother leaning against the wall and staring out through the barred windows.

Mickey slid a glance in his direction, and one corner of his mouth tugged upward. "Bill," he said, almost to himself. "This is quite a surprise!"

"Hi, Mickey. How're you doing?"

"Better. At least, *I* think I'm better. You'll have to check with Dr. Powell to get the official word on that."

"They treating you okay?"

"Sure." Winking, Mickey dropped his voice to a whisper. "They won't let me say that they don't. Have a seat. Sorry if the accommodations aren't up to your standards."

Bill sat on the edge of the single chair. "You look good, and you sound good—"

"You seem surprised."

"Well, the last time I saw you, things were a little . . ."

"Crazy? Wacko? Off the deep end?" Mickey supplied, his eyes shining.

"Out of touch," Bill said, feeling a little more at ease.

"Always the diplomat, eh, Doc?" Mickey countered. "So, what's up? Just a friendly chat about the weather?"

"Not really."

"I didn't think so." Mickey crossed his arms over his chest. "Shoot!" Then he laughed when Bill blanched slightly.

Bill gazed at him, his arm still aching from the bullet wound Mickey had put there only a couple weeks before.

"Sorry, bad choice of words."

"Real bad." Bill tried to find some hint of the brother he'd grown up with in this man standing before him. "Look, Mick, I had to come talk to you and see if we can clear the air. I know there must be a thousand things bothering you that you've got questions about. I think it's time we just talked."

Mickey eyed Bill. God, he was enjoying this, watching Bill squirm. "Maybe you're right."

"Okay—you start."

"Well, brother Bill . . . I guess that, since Michael isn't my son, my foremost concern is my daughter. How's she doing?"

Bill's muscles tensed. Didn't Mickey know that Melissa Phillips wasn't his daughter?

"I don't really know, but I think Melissa is fine."

"I'm not talking about Melissa. She's not my daughter anyway," Mickey said, waving away Bill's words. "I want to know how my new little baby, Jennifer, is doing."

"Who?"

"You know, Jennifer Rose."

Bill stared at him, stunned. "Why don't you sit down for a minute, Mickey? You're a little confused." Bill hesitated, then decided to set the record straight. "Jennifer Rose is *my* new baby."

Mickey refused to take a seat. Instead, he walked over to the closet and frowned into the mirror on the door. "Come on, Bill," he growled. "You were there at the hospital. Laura and I have finally had that little girl we wanted all our lives. She's going to be a beautiful blonde, just like her mother." Mickey's blue eyes clouded.

Bill was dumbstruck. He didn't like the shadows in Mickey's eyes. Something about his brother had turned dangerous, but Bill felt he couldn't back off. It was too important that Mickey understand what was real and what was fantasy. "Think for a minute, Mickey. You know that Laura is my wife now. You're married to Maggie."

Mickey's fingers touched the cool glass mirror, stroking it, but his cold eyes stared straight through Bill. The air was charged with electricity.

The orderlies were watching Mickey. "Is there a problem here?" one of them asked.

Mickey shook his head. "No problem at all."

"Good. Time's about up."

Mickey managed a smile. "Just forget about Jennifer for a while," he suggested.

"She's my daughter," Bill repeated.

Mickey's lips tightened, and he glanced down at Bill's hand. Abruptly, he asked, "How's the arm?"

"It's getting better," Bill said slowly.

Mickey sighed and rubbed his chin. "I still don't know how I did that to you, Bill. I just can't believe that I'm capable of such a thing. The mind is a very mysterious thing, don't you think?"

"Amen," Bill whispered. "Do you remember that night at all?"

"Vaguely. Bits and pieces, mainly. Like, I don't remember how I got to your house, but

I can remember being there with you and Dad," Mickey lied, staring straight into his brother's eyes. *Good old, perfect Bill. Just you wait, buddy boy.*

"What about Michael's accident? Do you remember being at Brookville Hospital with Maggie and Michael?" Bill pressed.

"Same thing. I can remember being in the waiting room with Maggie, but there are lots of holes, too many."

"Have you thought much about how we're going to handle Michael?"

Mickey avoided Bill's eyes. "I don't want to hurt Michael. I'll always consider him *my* son. I'm willing to do whatever everyone thinks is best."

Bill didn't really believe Mickey, but was relieved nevertheless. "Good! He's been asking a lot of questions about you, Mickey. He loves you very much."

"What have you told him about me?"

"We've explained that you've started to get your memory back and are confused about the past and the present. He knows that you're working with psychiatrists to try to get well. But we also told him that you just want to be alone for a while to sort things out."

"And he bought that?" Mickey didn't believe it for a minute.

"Most of it. But I can tell he's anxious to hear it from you—he doesn't completely believe us. We've told him that you're seeking psychiatric help to get you over the first few hurdles; other than that, he doesn't know anything, and his doctor would prefer that he be spared any shocks until he's completely recovered."

"Well, you can count on me," Mickey said with a smirk. "I think it's best if I just stay out of his life for a while longer. At least until I get things straightened out here."

"What does Dr. Powell say?"

Mickey shrugged. "Not a whole lot. We talked the other day and then last night. I think he might understand me a little better now. He's going to start me on regular therapy sessions in another day or two."

"That's good."

"Dr. Horton?" the taller orderly said, catching Bill's gaze. "Just a couple more minutes, okay?"

"Sure."

Bill turned back to his brother. "Well, Mick. Is there anything I can do for you? Maybe some questions I can answer?"

If only you knew. I've got all the answers. "Not right now."

"Okay, but whatever I can do for you, Mickey, just let me know. I want you to get well as soon as possible. We all do."

Mickey forced a calm smile. "Thanks."

"Good luck, Mick. I'll see you later." Bill clapped his brother on the back, then passed through the door with the orderlies.

"In hell," Mickey whispered, his blue eyes glinting as the dead bolts slipped into place. "I'll see you in hell."

Mickey flopped down on his bed and smiled coldly. Someday, he would kill his brother. And then he'd dance on Bill's grave!

He was still lying on his bed some time later when the locks clanged once again and the door swung inward. "Good morning, Mickey! How are you today?" Dr. Powell asked softly.

"Not too bad," Mickey replied.

Dr. Powell seated himself on the old chair. "I saw Bill a little while ago, and I wanted to see how your visit with him went."

"Didn't he tell you?"

"Yes. But I wanted your version." Dr. Powell settled back in his chair and pulled off the cap of his pen with his teeth.

The old fool. Mickey offered the doctor a crooked grin. "It went just fine."

"Did it?"

"Sure. I was glad that he stopped by to see me, especially since you said I couldn't have any visitors."

The doctor nodded. "Your brother can be very persuasive."

Right. Like with my wife. "I've been kind of concerned about his arm, but apparently he doesn't hold the accident against me," Mickey said.

"Should he?"

Shrugging, Mickey met the doctor's intense gaze. "I would understand if he did."

"He's your brother. That's not a tie one forgets very easily."

Yeah, Bill and I—just two peas in a pod. "I know."

"You opened the blinds," Dr. Powell observed, noticing the sunshine streaming into the room.

" 'Bout time, don't you think?"

"Yes. I hope that you can go outside soon, get some exercise."

Mickey stretched and groaned, looking through the bars longingly. "I'd like that."

"I think we're making progress. I'm going to bring in Dr. Foster this afternoon to meet you. I've arranged for him to start your therapy sessions tomorrow."

"I don't want Foster," Mickey said calmly.

"He's one of the best psychiatrists on staff and—"

"What about Laura?" Mickey demanded, sitting up straight, his eyes fixed on Dr. Powell.

"I don't think that would be a good idea to begin with."

"I do."

"Talk to Dr. Foster first, and then—"

"I don't want to talk to Dr. Foster. I want Laura. Did she say she wouldn't help me?"

"I didn't ask her," Dr. Powell said calmly.

"*What?* Did you ask Bill?"

"Considering everything—"

Mickey's face changed. "Just ask her, okay?"

Dr. Powell's mouth compressed to a thin line. "I'll decide who should be the one to work with you."

"Oh, no, you won't, doctor." Mickey planted his feet on the floor and pulled himself up to his full height. Towering over Dr. Powell, he smiled grimly. "I'll decide whom I'll talk to and when. Let's get that straight right now. I'm not going to see anyone until I have a chance to convince Laura to take my case."

"What if Laura refuses?" the doctor asked, ignoring the fire in Mickey's eyes.

"She won't."

"How can you be so sure? I'm certainly not going to encourage her."

"It doesn't matter what you do. I'll convince her!"

"Will you see Dr. Foster if Laura refuses?"

"You haven't been listening, have you? I'm not going to talk to anyone but Laura, no matter how long I have to wait. You can parade anyone you want through here, but I don't have to talk to them. I'll choose whom I'll open up to," he said, as calmly as if he were baiting a prosecutor in the courtroom. Just like the old Mickey Horton.

"Did you tell that to Bill?"

"No. I thought I'd go through the proper channels."

"Fair enough," Dr. Powell said, standing. He wanted to get through to Mickey, but he wasn't sure that Laura was the best way. "I'll be back later. I'll talk to Laura, but you have to understand that I can't make any promises."

Mickey's gaze grew distant, and he sat down on the bed.

"Don't shut me out, Mickey. It's important not to bottle anything up. You've got to let your feelings out."

Mickey rolled over and turned his back to Dr. Powell.

"Mickey?"

Clenching his teeth firmly together, Mickey built a wall of silence around himself. He heard Dr. Powell, but only faintly, and he didn't really give a damn what the man was saying to him. He just wanted to hide—until Laura came to see him. Songs from the past filled his head, and finally he didn't hear the doctor at all.

"Mickey!" Dr. Powell shook his head in defeat and left, locking the door behind him. Feeling manipulated, he walked slowly down the carpeted hallways to his office. He was tired and his head ached, and it was only ten in the morning. Groaning, he sifted through the pile of papers on his desk. "One of these days I'm going to straighten out this mess," he muttered, still lost in thought about Mickey Horton. When he finally found the file he wanted, he reached for the phone and dialed.

"University Hospital," a young receptionist replied.

"Dr. Laura Horton, please. This is Dr. Powell from Bayview."

"Just a minute, Dr. Powell. I'll connect you with her office."

The pause at the other end gave him time to stack some folders that had fallen to the floor. He knew that if he put them back on his desk, they'd be lost in no time.

"Dr. Powell?" Laura's clear voice came through the wire.

"Yes, Laura. I'm sorry to interrupt you so early in the day, but there's been an interesting development in your brother-in-law's case."

"Oh." Laura braced herself for bad news. "Is everything all right? Is Mickey hurt?"

"Oh, good heavens, no. Nothing like that. I didn't mean to alarm you. It's just that I've had an unusual request from Mickey concerning his therapy . . . he wants you to conduct the sessions."

Laura's stomach lurched. *"Me?* Are you sure?" What was Mickey up to?

"It surprised me, too. He mentioned it earlier, and I wasn't certain he was serious, but this morning he's rather adamant about it."

"What do you mean?"

"Well, he's refused to talk to Dr. Foster or to anyone else on staff until he has a chance to see you. He's convinced that he can persuade you to take the job."

Laura's palms began to sweat. She wasn't ready to face Mickey, not yet. But still, if it was his only chance to return to sanity . . . "I don't know what to say, Dr. Powell," she said, ignoring the easy excuses that leaped to mind. "Do you think it's a good idea?"

"To tell you the truth, no. I don't like it one bit. There was an incident a few days ago when he was visited by Linda Phillips."

Sighing, she leaned back in her chair, her hair straying out of the pins holding it away from her face. Linda Phillips always spelled trouble where Mickey was concerned. "It was bad, I take it."

"Very. He attacked her."

"Oh, dear God."

"Don't worry, she's all right. But he was making threats to you, as well."

Laura felt like crying, and the burden of guilt seemed to press heavily on her shoulders. What had she done to Mickey with all of her lies? "I don't see how I could help," she whispered.

"Neither do I—and I want to understand what triggers his violent episodes before I'll feel comfortable about exposing you to him. I told Mickey he should wait, but I'm pretty sure his mind is set. I don't think we can dissuade him."

"Are you saying I should see him?" Laura asked, trying to ignore the quivering in her stomach.

"Certainly not! I'm only telling you what happened here. I think you should discuss everything with Bill, and then maybe we should all get together and talk."

"I see."

"I'll continue working on Mickey to change his mind. And I'm still going to take Dr. Foster in to meet him this afternoon." He sighed. "Maybe together we can make some progress. I just wanted you to know what might be happening if we hit a roadblock."

"I appreciate that. And, yes, I'll discuss it with the other members of the family. If he's as set on this as you say he is, I might be his only chance, right?"

"That's possible. But I hope not."

"Oh, Lord . . ."

"Look, Laura, I don't want to alarm you prematurely. I just thought you should know."

"Thank you. Please don't mention the violence to Bill."

"I won't. But, Laura, I think you and Bill should talk this over, cover everything," Dr. Powell said, remembering Bill's request that his visit to Mickey be kept secret. "There have been too many lies and half-truths already."

"I know." Laura swallowed against a wave of guilt. Weren't her lies the reason for Mickey's insanity? Taking a deep breath, she pulled herself together, and her voice remained surprisingly steady. "Bill and I will call you late this afternoon to see how it went with Dr. Foster. If there's any change before then, please let me know."

"Certainly."

"Thanks for calling."

Laura hung up the phone and dropped her head into her hands. "Oh, God, what am I going to do?" she whispered, and her mind filled with memories of her unhappy marriage to Mickey. She knew that Bill would never let her be alone in the same room with Mickey, and considering his attack on Linda Phillips, she wasn't at all sure she wanted to either.

"I can't do it!" But she couldn't shake the guilt that clung to her like a cold, dark cloak.

"Do something, Laura," she told herself. "Don't just sit here sniveling." Setting her jaw, she sat up and thumbed through her appointment book, then called her receptionist on the intercom.

"Yes, Dr. Horton?"

"Do I have anyone coming in this afternoon?"

"No—we had this week and next cleared

because we expected you to be out having the baby," her receptionist replied.

"Thank goodness she came early," Laura said with a faint smile. "I think I'll go home."

"I would, if I had a darling baby like that."

"Thanks. And could you please get Bill on the phone?"

"I don't think so. He just left a message about ten minutes ago, saying that he'll be in surgery until early afternoon."

Laura tapped her pencil on the desk. "Okay, then leave a message for him to meet me at home as soon as he can get there— but please, tell him it's not an emergency. And leave the same message for my father-in-law."

"Will do," her receptionist said.

"Thanks." Laura tipped back in her chair and shook the hair out of her eyes. Would she be helping or hurting Mickey if she agreed to become his counselor? Closing her eyes, she wondered if this horrid nightmare would ever end.

Doug cut the engine and stared at Julie's house. Was she inside or did she stay with Don? With his teeth clamped together at the thought, Doug got out of the car and walked up the path leading to the front porch. He'd had a lousy night, and his morning had gone steadily downhill, but now he was determined to settle things with Julie once and for all. Just when, at long last, they could be together, his week in Chicago seemed to have driven him out of her mind.

He ignored the doorbell and chose to pound his fist against the heavy, hardwood door. It seemed like an eternity before it finally opened and there was Julie, looking at him with those wide, beautiful eyes that cut right through him.

"Hi," he said, offering a conciliatory smile.

"Doug." Her breath caught in her throat for a moment. "What are you doing here?"

"I just wanted to talk."

"I . . . I don't know if that would be such a good idea," she said, fighting the impulse to rush into his arms.

"Can I come in?"

"Maybe you should just go," she whispered. "We said everything we had to say last night."

Her attitude made him want to scream. He saw the reluctance in her eyes, and his blood started to boil. "No way. We're going to talk." He shoved open the door and stormed into the entry hall. Everything looked just the way it had when he'd left. The chandelier still gleamed, the grandfather clock still ticked softly, and all of Julie's half-finished portraits were stacked inside the door of the den. So what had changed?

"You shouldn't be here—"

"Don't tell me that," he said, whirling to face her. "Before I left, you were begging me to marry you, you were issuing ultimatums. I did everything I could to make that possible. Now I come home a free man and ask you to marry me, and I can't even get the time of day! What the hell is going on?"

Julie leaned back against the door. "Maybe *your* lack of interest the past couple of weeks made me do some thinking of my own," she said, her heart breaking. "Maybe you were right all along. We shouldn't rush into anything."

"Great!" Walking into the living room, Doug dropped onto the sofa and blew out a deep breath, trying to calm himself down. "If you're trying to make me jealous, Julie, you don't have to. I love you. I want you. I need you. What more do you want me to say?"

She stood in the archway, one shoulder pressed against the wall. He was so handsome, and his eyes held her, begged her to understand. Feeling herself weaken, she forced herself to remember Kim and the lies—all of the lies.

"We had something special," he insisted, his voice seductive.

"Once, maybe," she said, her throat burning.

"God, I love you."

"But that changes depending on whichever way the wind blows."

"You know that's not true!"

Julie shook her head and fought back her tears. "Do you remember your speech not too long ago? The one where you told me that *Kim* seemed to get along better with your daughter . . . *Kim* had accepted your past, something no one else ever had . . . *Kim* had stood by you when no one else did? Have I left anything out?"

He stood and crossed the room, stopping

only a few inches from her. He was so close that she could touch him, feel the warmth of his breath, smell the familiar scent of his cologne.

"Don't twist my words to use them against me," he warned. "You know how I feel. Do you want me to go back and dig up words that you've said in the past? The important thing is what we mean to each other, deep down inside. Can't you see that?"

Julie gazed into his eyes for a moment and then looked away. Sunlight from the window danced in her hair and caught in her tear-drenched eyes.

Doug leaned forward to kiss her, but she drew away. "Don't, please," she said hoarsely.

His hands caught her waist. "I came back from Chicago to tell you that I'm free. I'm done with Kim. All that's behind me, and all I want is to marry you and spend the rest of my life with you."

"That's this week."

"No! That's forever."

"Well, I'm not so sure about that. I've been doing a lot of soul-searching while you were gone. I'm not sure we've ever had a chance together." Dear God, why wouldn't he leave her alone? Being this close to him tore her apart.

"What's that supposed to mean?" he growled.

"There's never really been a time when there wasn't some outside influence keeping us apart. I'm starting to believe in fate."

Doug felt a chill race down his spine.

"Maybe you'd better spell it out for me, Julie. What're you trying to say?"

Her chin quivered. "I just think our time came and went, and we missed it. Don said—"

"I don't want to hear what that fool has to say," he cut in, stepping closer, feeling the warmth of her body, smelling the scent of her skin.

Julie's ragged emotions gave way to anger. "Don't you dare say anything bad about Don! He's been by my side helping me through all my troubles these past few days. And where were you? Shacked up with Kim in Chicago!"

"I didn't invite Kim."

"Liar!"

"Julie, please, just listen. I didn't even know she was going until she got on the plane. It was a total shock. And she wasn't staying with me in Chicago. You've *got* to believe me. That was her last-ditch attempt to win me back and break us up. Are you going to let her win?"

Julie inched away from him. "Please, Doug, just leave it alone. Okay? I don't think we have anything else to say to each other."

Frustrated, he reached out and captured her arm in his strong fingers. "Can we go out to dinner tonight and discuss this? Don't we owe ourselves that much after all we've shared?"

"I . . . I can't."

"Why not?"

"I already have plans."

"With?"

"Not that it's any of your business, but I'm having Don over tonight. He asked me out to celebrate something special, so I suggested we eat here," she said, feeling no satisfaction in flaunting Don in Doug's face.

Doug shook his head. "Don't make any foolish mistakes, Julie."

"I'm afraid I did before—when I fell for you," she whispered. "But that's over."

"No way!"

"Mom?" David walked into the room, carrying a duffel bag over his shoulder. He stopped short and his eyes darkened when he saw Doug. "Oh . . . I didn't mean to interrupt," he said, looking from his mother to Doug and back again. "I just wanted to tell you that I'm going to spend the night with the Grants. Paul called to say we're supposed to be back on the job tomorrow, and I don't want to be late. I'm already on thin ice with Bob."

"I don't know, David," she said doubtfully. "Your head . . ."

David flashed her an uneven grin. "It's fine, Mom. Besides, Paul's promoted me to the shipping department. I'm a clerk now— no more dock work. And Grandpa said I could take the bandage off today."

"That's wonderful. Well, as long as you're sure you're okay."

"I don't want to lose my job, okay? Bob is dying to find an excuse to fire me." David glanced at Doug. Working for Anderson Manufacturing was the best job he'd ever had. He didn't want to blow it—especially since he had one strike against him to start with. Bob Anderson was Julie's ex-husband.

"If you're sure you're up to it," she repeated.

"I'm fine, really. Maybe I should go now," he said, frowning at Doug.

"It's all right," Julie said hastily. "Doug was just leaving."

Doug eyed the boy, then glared at Julie. "He'll be gone all night. How convenient."

"Stop it!" she said, her face draining of color.

Rather than make a scene in front of Julie's son, Doug strode out of the house and heard the door shut sharply behind him. He stuffed his hands deep into his pockets and wondered why he loved Julie so much. She was driving him out of his mind. Kicking the loose stones on the path, he clenched his jaw against the bitter taste of rejection as he walked back to his car.

Chapter Six
Questions

Laura wiped a drip of milk from Jennifer's tiny lips. The baby yawned, closing her wide blue eyes.

"Looks like naptime," Laura said, just as the timer on the oven went off. Laying Jennifer in the bassinet near the kitchen table, she placed a quick kiss on the baby's forehead and then hurried back to turn off the timer and retrieve a batch of oatmeal cookies from the oven.

Ever since she'd gotten home from the hospital this morning, she'd tried to busy herself so that she wouldn't think of Mickey. Baking cookies had taken up some of the time.

As she was sliding the hot cookies onto wire racks to cool, she heard a car pull into the driveway. "Here we go," she murmured, bracing herself for what was sure to be a confrontation with her husband.

A few seconds later Bill walked into the kitchen. His smile was wide and his blue eyes twinkled as he wrapped his arms around his wife and kissed her hair. "Hi."

"Hi, yourself. How was surgery?"

"Fine," he said distractedly, not wanting to worry her. The truth of the matter was that, because of the pain in his arm, he hadn't been able to work in the operating room and his assistant had been forced to take over.

"Then everything's all right?" she asked, seeing the shadows in his eyes.

He shook off his black mood. "Except for one thing."

"What's that?"

"Well, the strangest thing happened today," he said with a wink.

You don't know the half of it, she thought. "What?"

"Well, after I was finished in surgery, I got this cryptic message from my receptionist." He let go of Laura to reach for a warm cookie. "Seems some beautiful blonde wanted me to come home and spend the rest of the afternoon with her."

"Is that right?" Laura laughed nervously.

"So, I figured it was one of two things."

"Oh?"

"Either this lady wanted me to carry her up to the bedroom and make love to her all afternoon and long into the night—"

"Dreamer," she cut in.

"Or . . ."

"Or what?"

"Or she wanted me to babysit my daughter

while she visited our son at Brookville Hospital." He took a bite of his cookie and walked over to the bassinet. "Either way, the answer is yes." He touched Jennifer's cheek, and the baby cooed.

"It's not quite that pleasant," Laura mumbled.

"No?"

"It's Mickey."

Bill's shoulders stiffened, and he turned to face her. "I should have guessed." He dropped into one of the kitchen chairs and frowned. "What happened?"

"Dr. Powell called me this morning. Mickey's refusing his help. He won't begin therapy sessions."

Bill's jaw tightened, and he avoided Laura's eyes. "I suppose I should have expected something like this."

"Why?"

"Because it's all my fault!" He slammed his fist on the table, then sighed and wearily rubbed his eyes. "I shouldn't have seen him this morning."

"You went out to Bayview?"

"Yes."

"But, when? Why? I had no idea—"

"I didn't want to tell anyone before I went."

"Not even me?"

"Especially not you. I didn't want to worry you."

"Bill," she said reproachfully, pouring him a cup of coffee and placing it on the table. "No secrets. Remember?"

"I know . . . but I really thought that

Mickey and I needed to talk to each other—
you know, man to man, brother to brother. I
felt that if we cleared the air between us, it
would help resolve everything. Looks like I
was wrong." Scowling, he took a long drink
from his cup.

"Maybe," she said, sitting down across
from him. "But it doesn't matter now. What's
done is done."

"Doesn't make me feel any better."

"So, tell me about it," she suggested, cradling her cup between her hands. "What did
you think, while you were there? How did it
go?"

"I actually thought it went pretty well.
Mickey seemed glad to see me. He acted like
he was sorry about shooting me, and he
talked very lucidly, just like the old Mickey."

"The old Mickey you saw in court at his
hearing," she reminded him, a chill of fear
sliding down her spine. She'd heard how
cold and calculating Mickey had been during
the sanity hearing.

"Exactly. So I really don't know what
could have happened. The only thing I can
think of is—" He broke off as they heard the
sound of a car door slamming.

Laura peeked through the curtains. "It's
your dad. I asked him to stop by. Don't
bother," she said as Bill started to get up. "I'll
let him in." Hurrying from the kitchen, she
opened the door just as Tom was approach-
ing the front porch.

"I got a message that you wanted to see
me," he said, following Laura down the hall

to the kitchen. "Mmm. Smells good in here."

"Thanks. Help yourself." She placed a platter of cookies on the table.

"So you did leave a message with my secretary?"

"Yes," Laura said, glancing nervously at Bill. "There's something I want to talk to you about."

"It's Mickey, isn't it?" Tom asked, the lines in his face deepening.

"Yes."

The older man sighed and his brow furrowed. "I knew it." Then, nodding to Bill, he walked across the room to peer into the bassinet. As he looked at Jennifer, some of the worry eased from his face. "And how is my new granddaughter?"

"Growing every day," Laura replied, pouring him a cup of black coffee and adding a teaspoon of sugar.

"You know, she's the best thing that's happened to this family in a long time," Tom said thoughtfully. "Oh, thanks." He took the cup Laura offered and sat down next to his son. "Now, before we start in on Mickey, tell me about Michael."

"He should be home in a few days, unless there are complications," Bill said. "I looked at his chart when we visited him; he's fine."

"Thank God," Tom said fervently. "And how is he taking the news about Mickey?"

Bill leaned back in his chair. "Not too well. He's asking lots of questions. But we've managed to avoid letting out the fact that Mickey's in the sanitarium. We don't want to worry him—

not until he's out of the woods himself."

"Okay. So, what's with Mickey? Is he all right?"

Laura nodded. "Yes. I mean, I think so. No physical problems, at least. As I just started to tell Bill, Dr. Powell called me a while ago and told me that Mickey was refusing all staff help with his therapy sessions. He's refusing to see anyone . . . but me."

"What!" Bill tensed. What the hell was going on?

"You didn't give me a chance to finish before you jumped in, blaming yourself, honey," Laura said gently. Turning to Tom, she explained, "Bill went out to see Mickey this morning."

"And he seemed fine," Bill said.

The lines around Tom's mouth deepened.

"As I was telling Laura, he seemed concerned and sorry about hurting me, and spoke very lucidly, except once." Bill glanced at the bassinet. "He asked me how his daughter was . . . and he meant Jennifer."

"Jennifer?" Laura nearly dropped her cup.

"Right. He told me all about how you and he had always wanted a little girl, and now he had one—a beautiful blonde, like her mother."

Tom asked, "What did you tell him?"

"I thought the best thing to do was just insist on the truth. I told him to stop and think for a minute. I explained that I was married to Laura now, and that Jennifer was *my* daughter. I reminded him that he was married to Maggie."

"What did he say?"

"He just brushed the subject aside, and started talking about something else."

"Doesn't sound good," Tom muttered.

"I shouldn't have gone up there."

Laura reached across the table and took her husband's hand. "Don't take the blame for his change in attitude. There's really no way you can predict the mood swings in a psychotic mind."

"What does Cliff Powell want to do?" Tom asked his daughter-in-law.

Laura squeezed Bill's hand. "He left it up to me."

Bill's eyes sparked. "You didn't tell him you'd do it?"

"No, but—"

"There's no way I'll let you work with him!" Bill said emphatically. "After what he did to me, I'm not letting you anywhere near him."

"I think Bill's right, Laura. We need some kind of evidence that he's stabilized," Tom agreed.

"But there's no way to get that kind of proof. At least, not until he's well into the therapy sessions and an accurate diagnosis has been made." Laura's fingers tightened on her husband's hand.

"You can't be serious," he said. "You've got Michael to worry about, and Jennifer. You can't take on Mickey, too."

"Maybe I should go talk to him about this," Tom suggested.

Laura shrugged her shoulders. "Dr. Powell

said he was going to take Dr. Foster in to see Mickey this afternoon. He's going to call me later and tell me if there's been any change. We might as well sit tight until we hear what they've come up with. Mickey might make another about-face."

"And if he doesn't?" Tom stared at his daughter-in-law.

Bill's lips were a thin line. "It doesn't matter. I'm not going to let her do it!"

"Do you know what you're saying?" Tom asked quietly. He looked suddenly old, and his eyes filled with pain. Mickey was as much his son as Bill.

"I don't trust my brother alone with my wife. I don't think he's ready for that."

"But if he is adamant about this, and if you withhold Laura's help from him, you might be condemning him to life in a sanitarium."

Bill scraped his chair back and walked to the window. He couldn't let Mickey ruin his family. "Come on, Dad. He might snap out of this completely on his own. Right, Laura?"

"Anything is possible, but the prospects of that happening are pretty remote. Unless someone gets in there and helps him bring all his psychoses to the surface, I don't like to think of his chances."

"They're as good as anyone else's," Bill said stubbornly.

"I'm going to help him, Bill," she said quietly.

"Laura—"

"I have to." She lifted her chin defiantly. "I feel responsible."

"For God's sake, Laura—"

"And so do you! You said so earlier—you thought your visit triggered something in him. I know you don't like it, Bill, but this is something I have to do."

Tom checked his watch. "Look, I've got to run back to the hospital for rounds. There's nothing more I can say until we hear from Dr. Powell."

"Well, I'm not about to sit around here and wait," Bill said decisively. A muscle jumped in his jaw. "I'm going out there right now!"

Laura shook her head. "Please, honey, just wait. The doctor said he'd call—"

"No way! I want to know what's going on. I can't believe that they let the patients dictate treatment!"

"You can't just go storming up there, making all sorts of demands," Laura exclaimed.

"The hell I can't! I'll see you later." Bill grabbed his jacket and stormed out the back door.

"Bill!" Laura called, nearly stumbling as she scrambled up and tried to follow him. Jennifer started to cry, and Tom caught Laura's arm, holding her back. "Let him go, Laura. Maybe it's the best thing for him to go out and talk to Dr. Powell. He'll get a better feel for what they're talking about, what's going on. This is as hard for him as it is for the rest of us."

"But I can't—"

"Shh."

The baby continued to cry, and Laura, worried sick about her husband picked up

the child and held her close. "It's all right,"
she whispered into the down-soft hair. She
leaned against the counter and watched
through the open door as Bill jumped into
his sports car and roared out of the driveway.

"He has to handle this his own way," Tom
said softly.

"I hope you're right," Laura whispered, a
shiver of dread sliding down her spine as she
looked out at the snow melting in the yard.
Icicles had begun to drip and break from the
roof gutters. "I sure hope you're right!"

Salem's roads were slick. The snow was
beginning to melt into slippery slush, which
often hid the patches of ice still clinging to
the pavement.

Bill pressed down on the accelerator and
his tires spun and slid on the slippery surface
as he sped toward Bayview.

What was Mickey's game? He downshifted
and tried to think of some sane reason why
Mickey would want Laura for his doctor. But
he couldn't. And Mickey wasn't sane. Bill
couldn't forget the hatred so clear on his face
when Mickey had pointed the gun at him
and fired.

The image was so vivid that he didn't
notice the red station wagon as it ran the
stop sign until it was right in his path.

"God Almighty!" Slamming on the brakes,
Bill yanked at the steering wheel; the tires
locked and the car skewed wildly. He
pounded on the horn and then pumped the
brakes, swerving at the last possible instant.

His little car shuddered as it careened through the intersection sideways, nearly sideswiping the red wagon.

"Dear God," Bill whispered, trying desperately to regain control. His car jumped the curb near a service station, crashed through a signboard and spun recklessly toward the gas pumps.

"No!" Standing on the brakes, Bill wrenched the steering wheel to the side. Pain seared up his wounded arm, and the car skidded into the island, the tires bouncing off the concrete barrier, and finally stopped with a thud.

Badly shaken, Bill couldn't even summon the strength to open the door. "Oh, God," he whispered over and over again as a couple service station attendants ran over to the car and jerked open the driver's door. Climbing out of his car, Bill was still trembling, his knees weak, his wounded arm throbbing.

"Hey, Mac, you all right?" an attendant in navy-blue coveralls asked anxiously.

"I think so."

The attendant let out a long whistle. "You were lucky. Doesn't look like the car's got a scratch."

"Incredible," Bill murmured, rubbing his arm and trying to get his bearings. "I . . . I'm sorry about—"

"Don't worry about it. Lucky no one was getting gas."

Bill cringed at the thought of slamming into another car parked at the island. "At least I can pay you for the sign." He looked at the splintered boards littering the tarmac, around which a little crowd of onlookers had gathered. The red car and its driver were nowhere in sight.

"Don't worry about no money," the attendant said, waving away Bill's offer. "That old sign's been hit so many times, I can't count 'em. I'm just glad you're okay."

Bill helped him pick up the pieces of wood, and then, after insisting that the man take twenty dollars, he got back in his car and slowly pulled out onto the highway. All of his anger was gone. He was just glad to be alive.

By the time he arrived at Bayview, he had stopped shaking; even though he was calm again, he was more determined than ever to protect his family.

A few minutes later he was seated across from Dr. Powell in the psychiatrist's small, cluttered office.

"I take it that Laura talked to you," Powell said, lighting his pipe.

"Right."

"Then you know about Mickey's request?"

Bill tented his fingers under his chin and nodded. "Laura made it sound more like a demand. I want to know what the hell is going on out here, Powell. Since when do the patients set the ground rules? I can't believe that—"

"Hold on, Bill. You're jumping to conclusions."

"According to my wife, Mickey is refusing therapy unless it's with her."

"That was his demand this morning. It will probably change."

"It damn well better!"

Dr. Powell frowned and puffed on his pipe. "I think you should calm down, doctor. You're getting yourself all worked up over nothing."

"Over nothing! You call this whole situation nothing?"

"I didn't mean it that way. I understand the trauma that you and your family are going through. But right now, the important person to consider is Mickey. If we can help him get back on track, so that he's the old, sane Mickey Horton, wouldn't that be the cure for a lot of the problems between you and Laura?"

Bill snorted. "I suppose so."

"Then let's just take this one step at a time. The first one is Mickey's demand that Laura be his counselor."

"Out of the question!"

"I tend to agree with you," Dr. Powell said thoughtfully. "I don't think it would be a good idea, but I have to think of my patient first."

Bill was suspicious. "Then what's this all about?"

"I just thought your family should know."

Bill relaxed a little. "How did it go with Dr. Foster?"

"Not very well, I'm afraid. Your brother wouldn't respond to anything Dr. Foster tried. Mickey just withdrew into his shell and sat there silently."

"You think it's an act?"

"I wish I knew."

Bill steeled himself and met the psychiatrist's gaze. "Do you think my visit this morning might have triggered this?"

"Hard to say—but, no, I doubt it."

"So, what are you going to do?" Bill asked, slightly relieved.

"What did you and Laura decide? Does she want to help?"

"Of course she does, but she's not convinced that she wouldn't be more harm than good for him. She blames herself for a lot of his problems." He leaned closer to the desk. "But I can't let her risk her life in an attempt to help Mickey. I still think my brother might be dangerous."

Dr. Powell nodded. "Then we're at an impasse. The question is; can you and your family get on with your lives if Mickey refuses anyone's help but Laura's?"

"I don't know," Bill said, his shoulders slumping. "I just don't know."

Don Craig was nervous, more nervous than he'd ever been in the courtroom. The butterflies in his stomach, coupled with the annoying sweatiness of his palms, made him realize that he was counting too much on this date. He'd gone out with Julie for several nights in a row, but tonight felt different. Tonight, he couldn't slow his heartbeat or think of anything but her.

After he'd pulled his car into her driveway, Don glanced into the rearview mirror to double-check his appearance. Then he grinned sheepishly and got out of the car.

"What's the matter with you, Craig? You're acting like a high-school kid!" he muttered as he climbed the front steps and rang the doorbell.

Within seconds, Julie opened the door. "About time you showed up, counselor."

"Am I late?"

"No, but I've been waiting," she teased, trying to forget the fact that, only hours before, Doug had been standing just where Don was now. "Come in, come in! It's still freezing out there!" She focused all of her attention on Don, ignoring her treacherous thoughts, and kissed him lightly on the cheek. "Make yourself at home. I've got to check on dinner. Why don't you fix us a drink, and I'll be right back."

"You've got yourself a deal," he said, watching her walk down the hall, keenly aware that he was head over heels in love with her. "Where's David?" he asked.

"Spending the night with some friends," she said over her shoulder, and then disappeared into the kitchen.

Don walked into the living room and crossed to the bar. As he gently stirred the martinis in a glass pitcher, he quelled all of his doubts about his relationship with Julie. The showdown with Doug had bothered him, but even though Doug was back in town, Julie seemed happy about tonight. He felt more lighthearted than he had in weeks as he poured two drinks.

He found Julie in the kitchen, standing on

tiptoes and reaching for a platter from a high cupboard. "Here, let me get that for you." Setting the drinks on the counter, he pulled down the dish, then grinned at Julie. "Looks like you could use a man around the house," he said.

"Or platform shoes," she teased, taking the drink he offered and sipping the dry martini. "Besides, David considers himself a man."

"Does he?"

"It won't be long," she sighed, "until he'll want to be on his own again. I'll hate to see him leave, but that's all part of being a mother, right?"

"Right. You've got to let him go." There was a long silence and Don finally said, "I suppose you've heard from Doug today."

Julie's heart skipped a beat, but she forced a smile. "Yes. He, uh, stopped by earlier."

"So, how'd it go?"

"Not great," she admitted, taking another sip of her drink. She decided to be completely honest with Don. She couldn't handle another relationship built on evasions and lies. "I realized while he was here that I don't trust anything he says anymore."

"How did he explain Kim being in Chicago?"

"I didn't really give him a chance. I found that I wasn't very interested." She cleared her throat. "I asked him to leave shortly after he got here because I wanted to start getting ready for tonight."

"Really?"

"Yes."

Don held her gaze, searching her eyes. He knew that she must still care for Doug, if only a little. "I don't want to say anything bad about Doug Williams, Julie. But I've seen how he's hurt you over and over again. Maybe he didn't intend to, but I can't help wondering if you two were ever meant to be with each other."

"Who knows? It really doesn't matter anymore, does it?"

Don took her glass and set it on the counter beside his, then wrapped his arms around her slim waist. He wanted nothing more than to kiss her, make love to her, hold her and never let go. But she'd hurt him once before—this time he wanted to be sure. He looked at her skeptically. "You're sure?"

She tried to be as honest as she could. "I've been doing a lot of thinking about that, Don," she whispered. "Believe me, this hasn't been easy for me. I feel one way one minute, another way the next."

"And?"

"And it's over," she said, feeling a painful constriction in her heart.

Don gently cupped her cheek with his palm. Then he encircled her neck with his fingers, drawing her face close to his. "I'll always be there for you, Julie, if you want me to be," he promised.

His eyes were so honest, his voice so kind. Julie swallowed hard. "I do."

Don pressed his lips to hers, gently at first, and then more eagerly when he felt her respond. Her arms lifted, and she clasped her fingers behind his neck. When he raised his head to stare at her, he couldn't fight the fire burning deep in his heart. "I love you so much."

"And I love you, Don," she said, her voice breathless.

His heart pounded; he pulled her close. Drunk with the scent and feel of her, he was completely lost. "I want you."

"And I want you."

His voice was ragged as he tried to hold onto his self-control. "Not just now, Julie, I'm talking about forever! I've felt this way about you since the first day I met you. I love you. I always have."

She believed him. His brown eyes were desperately sincere and his lips trembled slightly.

"If you want me, just say the word, Julie. Will you marry me?"

Wrapping her arms around his neck, she pulled his head back down to hers and tried not to think about Doug. She smiled, placing kisses on his face. "Yes, I'll marry you, Don Craig."

Chapter Seven

Turn the Page

Julie slowly opened her eyes and smiled. Sunshine was streaming in through her bedroom window, and she smelled the aroma of fresh-perked coffee wafting up from the kitchen. She rolled over and found a note on the pillow next to her.

Blinking her eyes into focus, she read the hastily scrawled words:

Dearest Julie,
Duty called. I had an early court time and didn't want to wake you. There's coffee brewing in the kitchen. Thanks for making me the happiest man in the world. I'll call you later.

Love you,
Don

"And I love you, too," she whispered. But her throat tightened at a fleeting memory of

Doug. "Just forget him," she said, hating herself. Don was the kindest, most loyal man she'd ever met, and she vowed she would make him a good wife. "Even if it kills me!"

Throwing back the sheets, Julie reached for her robe and walked downstairs. The house was quiet and lonely. Pouring herself some of Don's coffee, she squared her shoulders and raised her cup. "Here's to a new life!" *Without Doug Williams!* she added silently.

She'd just finished her breakfast when the phone rang. Probably Don, she thought, grinning impishly. "Good morning, counselor," she said, her voice low.

There was a pause, then a heavy sigh on the other end of the line. "Julie, I have to talk to you," Doug said quietly.

Julie wanted to die. "I don't think we have much to say right now," she said hurriedly, her back pressed against the wall.

"Listen, I just want you to hear me out. I think I deserve that much, after all we've been through. Will you meet me for lunch?"

Julie swallowed. How could she ever face Doug again? "I don't know. . . ."

"Please."

Her heart wrenched, and she decided that, in all fairness, she should at least tell Doug that she'd decided to marry Don. "All right," she said, her voice shaky.

"Good."

She cringed at the relief in his voice.

"Can you come to the club around noon?"

"Okay, noon it is."

"Julie . . . I love you."

Don't say that, Doug, please! Dying inside, Julie hung up without answering and leaned heavily against the wall.

It took all of her willpower not to call him back and cancel. She hurried upstairs and turned on the shower, all the while praying that Don wouldn't call before she could leave the house. She knew her voice would betray her, and she needed time to pull herself together. Collapsing against the cold tiles, she waited for the warm water to soothe her tense muscles.

"Well, it's now or never," she told herself finally, turning off the spigots.

After dressing quickly and writing a note to David, she drove downtown to window-shop and kill some time before she had to face Doug. But the dresses in the department stores and boutiques didn't hold her interest, and the hours passed slowly as she checked her watch every few minutes. Finally, it was time.

Nostalgia overwhelmed her as she entered Doug's Place. It was like walking through episodes of her life all over again, and she had to push the painful memories steadfastly aside.

Doug was in his office, counting receipts from the night before. He looked up immediately when she approached the doorway, and his face broke into a wide grin. "I thought maybe you'd changed your mind," he said, locking the cash in the safe.

"I said I'd be here."

"I know. But ever since I've been back, you've been hard to read."

"I thought I'd made myself clear. At least, I've tried to."

Pushing back his chair, he stood and stretched, then approached her. He tried to put his arm around her waist, but she slipped away and went to take a seat in a quiet booth away from most of the lunch crowd.

Sliding onto the padded bench opposite hers, Doug thought she was the most beautiful woman in the world. Her blue eyes avoided his, and her hands were shaking as she toyed with a napkin on the table. "Thanks for coming," he said softly.

"As you said, I guess I owe you this much. We do need to talk." Her voice was firm and emotionless, but she couldn't meet his gaze.

"Can I get you anything? Lunch? A drink?"

"No, thanks," she said with a trembling smile. "I think we'd better just talk and get this over with."

Doug's brows drew down into a frown. He clasped his hands together on the table and leaned forward. "Okay," he said slowly. "But I want you to just listen and hear me out. I knew nothing about Kim going to Chicago until I was sitting on the plane and she got on. I would never have—"

"Stop!" Julie couldn't stand to hear any more excuses. Swallowing hard, she whispered, "It's really not important. Not anymore."

"It is if you won't listen to me. I've been trying to tell you, the divorce is final. There's nothing holding us back from getting married. Isn't that what you've been waiting for?"

"Maybe it was."

His jaw clenched. "Was?"

"Yes. Past tense. I tried to tell you yesterday morning . . . our time came and went, and we missed it. I think it would be a big mistake for us to try to ignore everything that's happened and just blithely go on and get married."

"You're not serious—"

"Oh, Doug, I've never been more serious about anything in my life," she whispered, fighting tears again.

"I don't believe it. I love you. I know you love me. That's all that's important."

Shaking her head slowly, Julie said, "I *did* love you, Doug."

"Now, wait a minute! Don't try to tell me that you don't still love me. Look me in the eye, and tell me that you won't always love me."

Julie looked into his eyes, then glanced away, through the windows across the room. "I'm afraid it's gone way beyond that now, Doug. I've done a lot of thinking while you were gone. I've tried to pinpoint what's really important to me. I want a man I can depend on, a man who I know loves me and will do anything for me, a man I can love and respect and count on being there for me."

Doug's face hardened. "You're not talking about me, are you?"

"No. The man I'm talking about has been there for me all along. I was just too foolish to recognize it."

"Oh, God."

Forcing her eyes back to his, she said, "I'm going to marry Don Craig!"

"No!" Doug reached forward, grabbed her hands. "You can't."

"I can, and I will," she said slowly. "Don has asked me to marry him. I've given this a great deal of thought, and I've decided it's time to put all this behind me and get on with a new life, with a clean slate. He loves me, and I love him. It's as simple as that."

"Get serious, Julie. You don't love Don Craig!" Doug said, his temper getting control of his tongue. He was tired of Julie's games.

"Don't you tell me who I love! I don't think you've ever known the meaning of the word." She started to rise, but he pulled her back down into her chair.

"And don't *you* tell me that you don't love me—more than anything in your life. That kind of love doesn't just die."

"No, it doesn't," she agreed, lifting her chin. "It has to be killed."

"I can't believe that, after all we've shared, you'd fall for that spineless wimp."

Julie yanked her hands free of his. "Don's more of a man than you'll ever be."

"Ha! What kind of lies has he been feeding you anyway? How could he turn you against me in such a short time?"

"This has been coming for a long time, Doug. Looking back now, I see that it should have happened years ago."

"And it didn't because you love me. Admit it, Julie—you're using him to hurt me. You're punishing me for the fact that I never told you about Kim," he said, his eyes blazing. "You'll never marry Don."

Overcome by a flash of fury, she slapped him, hard.

Doug stood and leaned over the table, his eyes narrowing in anger. "That's what's really bothering you—admit it!"

"That's ridiculous! I'm not punishing you . . . and I'm not using Don. I love him, whether you believe it or not!"

"It'll never work. Sooner or later—maybe not today, maybe not next week—you're going to realize that you were meant for me. You can't marry him."

Julie answered him through clenched teeth. "I'm not only going to marry him, Doug, but I'm going to be the best wife in the world to him. I'll do anything to make him happy and keep our marriage together. Even if it kills me!" She winced at the hard sound of her words.

"It will!"

"Then so be it! I'm through, Doug. I've tortured myself for the last time over you. I'll never interfere in your life again!"

Balancing on his knuckles, Doug glowered at her, his face inches from hers, but Julie refused to budge. She returned his penetrating glare with one of her own and felt a strength she'd never known she had.

"Don't do this, Julie. It's the biggest mistake you'll ever make," he warned, his eyes softening.

"Not my biggest, Doug. My biggest was loving you, trusting you, believing all those lies you told me."

"If you think I'm going to beg, you're wrong. I won't."

"Good."

His eyes glittered dangerously. "You've played this hand out as far as it will take you. You'd better hope that I'm still around when you come back to your senses."

"If I were you, I wouldn't hold my breath. Good-bye, Doug Williams . . . or whatever your name really is," she said, her voice breaking as she moved blindly toward the door. A small part of her wanted him to give chase, and she half expected him to grab her from behind. But he didn't, and in a couple minutes, she was behind the wheel of her car racing out of the parking lot.

Doug watched her leave and finally realized that she was serious. It was over—unless he did something. Fast.

"Two can play this game," he decided. He walked to the phone on the bar and dialed directory assistance.

"What city, please?"

"Chicago. I need the number of the Town Center Hotel in Chicago," he said. Waiting anxiously, he stared at his reflection in the mirror behind the long, mahogany bar, then jotted down the number the operator gave him.

Dialing again, he felt better than he had since he'd returned to Salem. His lips twisted into a smile as the hotel's desk clerk answered.

"Town Center."

"Yes . . . would you please ring Kim

Douglas's room? I've forgotten what room she's in."

The connection seemed to take forever. Doug waited anxiously, his fingers drumming nervously on the bar.

"Hello?"

"Kim? It's Doug."

"Doug! You're the last person I expected to hear from! I've missed you something horrible," she admitted.

"Good," he said, running a hand over his chin, "because I want you to come back to Salem. I need to see you and talk to you."

"Is there something wrong?" she asked, her voice taking on a colder note. "Aren't you married to Julie yet?"

"No. Far from it. That's what I want to talk to you about. I'll be glad to buy your ticket and have it waiting for you at the airport. Will you come back?"

She hesitated just a second. There was a new note in her voice. "Didn't I tell you I'd always be there for you, Doug?"

"And I appreciate it. Look, I'll make the arrangements and get back to you. Talk to you later." He hung up the phone and leaned against the bar. A smile crept across his face, and he grinned at himself in the mirror. Julie Anderson was in for the surprise of her life!

Alice refilled the coffeepot and carried it from the kitchen to the living room, where the tension seemed to be mounting by the second.

Laura was seated on the couch near little Jennifer Rose, who was lying on her back

and kicking her legs at the ceiling. Tom sat
on the edge of his recliner; he looked like a
bundle of nerves.

"Laura? Another cup?" Alice offered.

"Yes, please."

"Tom, what about you?"

"What? Oh, sure," he said, forcing a tired
smile. He'd been a million miles away, wor-
rying about Mickey.

"Okay," Alice said, picking up the baby
and holding her close. "Where were we?"

Laura's lips curved down. "Back at square
one, I'm afraid. We still need to find a way
to convince Bill to let me try to help Mickey.
We'll never be able to live with ourselves if
we don't give him a chance."

"That's not going to be easy," Tom said.
"He was dead set against it yesterday. And
his meeting with Dr. Powell didn't do anything to change his mind."

"I just don't understand how a man can
turn his back on his own brother," Alice said
with a sigh.

"He's not," Tom pointed out. "Laura is
Bill's wife, and he's afraid Mickey might hurt
her. A man's wife comes before all others. I
wouldn't feel any differently, you know."

"Then it's up to me to convince him that
I'm in no danger from Mickey," Laura said.

Tom ran a weary hand over his face. "If
you're sure that this is what you want to do."

"Of course it is!" Alice said. She patted the
baby's back and smiled as her newest grand-
child gave a healthy burp. "She looks just
like you, Laura!"

"Don't say that to Bill!" Laura warned jokingly and leaned back against the couch. She became serious as she heard the kitchen door slam.

Bill walked into the room. He knew why he'd been summoned to his parent's house but figured he'd let them fill him in. His blue eyes pinned his wife. "What's up?"

"You know what we're talking about. The only way to clear up this problem with Mickey is for me to go and see him."

"Seems as if you've already made up your mind." He took off his coat and reached for Jennifer. "You've got one stubborn mother, little lady."

"I *have* made up my mind," Laura said.

"And you have a pretty stubborn mother as well," Alice said, eyeing her son.

Bill handed Jennifer back to Alice and his eyes passed over the members of his family. "And of course everyone backs Laura up. Right?"

"We have a lot at stake here," Tom began. "Mickey isn't the only one we have to think about. What happens when Michael finally visits him? He'll be devastated! Who knows what Mickey will do or what he'll reveal." Tom looked pointedly at his son. "We can't keep Michael away forever, and we have to be sure—absolutely sure—of Mickey's sanity first. We've got to do whatever we can to get Mickey back. I'm not talking about sacrificing Laura, of course. I just think there's got to be a way for her to work with him safely, so that all of our concerns are met."

"Bravo," Bill said. "Great speech, Dad, but it's my wife we're talking about."

"We know that," Alice cut in, her lips whitening. "But don't forget why Mickey's in that horrid sanitarium in the first place. We put him there because his mind snapped when he found out that you were Michael's father. You lied to him for years!"

"So it's my fault?" Bill said harshly, remembering the night all those years ago—the night he'd raped his brother's wife. Sick with disgust, he glanced across the room to the fireplace. A family portrait hung proudly over the mantel.

Alice fought back tears. "No, I'm not saying that anyone's to blame, but please, just listen to your father."

"Why did I know that you'd be in Mickey's corner?" Bill asked.

Alice glared at her son. "I'm thinking of you, too."

"Tell me about it."

"You and Laura need a stable home life now. Jennifer is going to demand much of your time and create lots of new pressures. It's time to simplify the outside distractions. We need Michael to know that you're his real father. We need Mickey out of Bayview and back in his life—with Maggie, we hope. We need—"

Bill had heard enough. "I know. Damn . . . I know, I know, I know. It doesn't look like I have much say in this, does it?"

"We have to help him," Laura said firmly.

Tom stood and clasped Bill's arm. "I knew you'd never turn your back on your brother."

"It's never been a question of that, Dad," Bill snapped. "But my first concern was, and still is, Laura. I'll agree to let Laura work with Mickey under one condition: I want to tell Mickey the circumstances of Michael's conception. I don't want him to think that Laura was ever sneaking around behind his back. I'd feel safer—maybe any antagonism he feels toward her will diminish. He needs to know the truth as much as anyone."

Laura blanched.

"Son, I don't think—"

"I mean it, Dad!"

"Then I want to be there with you," Laura declared. "He's going to need to hear some of those things from me."

Bill hesitated, but saw the determination in her eyes. "Okay. That'll give *me* a chance to see how he's responding to you. If I'm not convinced that he means no harm and that he fully respects you as a woman and a doctor, the deal is off."

"I think you should include Dr. Powell in your meeting, so there's an impartial observer," Tom suggested.

"I'm sure he'll insist anyway, but that's a good point," Laura agreed. "Bill and I might be too close emotionally to pick up on some of Mickey's reactions."

"Are you sure you can handle this?" Alice asked.

"Yes," Laura said, smiling at her baby, "I have to. For all of us."

"What about Maggie?" Tom asked.

"I'll talk to her," Alice said. "She's a level-headed girl. She wants to help Mickey as much as we do."

Tom asked, "So, what's the next step?"

"The sooner we get going on this, the better, as far as I'm concerned," said Bill. "I'll take Laura out there the day after tomorrow, and we'll have it out with Mickey. If things go well, I assume she'll start his sessions on Monday. Right, Laura?"

"Yes. That would be about right."

"Good," Tom said wearily. "Then it's settled. I feel like we're finally making progress."

Sitting up in his hospital bed, Michael stared at the phone he'd placed in his lap. Beneath it lay the newspaper article, the picture of Mickey staring up mockingly at him.

No one had bothered to tell him the truth, not even his own mother. Clenching his teeth firmly together, he dialed and waited for Maggie to answer.

"Hi, Maggie. It's Michael."

"Michael," she said, her voice cheerful, "how are you? Is everything okay?"

He bit at his lower lip. "I . . . I don't know. That's why I called you."

"What's wrong?"

"I want to know about Dad. I haven't been able to get any straight answers from anyone."

"Mickey is going to be fine, Michael. He needs some time to—"

"Stop! Maggie . . . I've heard all that. Maybe it would help if you'd tell me why he's been committed."

Maggie drew a swift breath. "What?"

"I saw the newspaper. There's an article about Dad. Why hasn't anyone said anything to me?"

"Oh, Michael! I'm so sorry. I didn't want to lie to you. I didn't want to hide anything from you. Everyone agreed that we should wait until we were sure you were strong enough before we told you."

So it was true! He sank back on the pillows. "Now's the time," he said.

"I don't know where to start."

"The beginning is always the best."

Maggie would have preferred to be there in person. She didn't want to tell him the news over the phone. But she could tell by his cold voice that he would demand answers—if not from her, then from someone else.

"The beginning was probably when he first suffered his amnesia, Mike. But the night of your accident is when everything went crazy."

"Funny you should put it that way."

"I'm sorry. . . . Mickey and I were sitting in the waiting room at the hospital, worried sick and waiting for some word on you. He started to get memory flashbacks," she said, omitting the fact that Mickey had discovered Michael wasn't his son. "He seemed to get very disoriented, and there was a pained look on his face. The next thing I knew, he took off. He just left me there at the hospital."

"What happened then?"

"From what I've been told and been able to piece together, he drove to Salem. First, he went to see Linda Phillips, and that evidently pushed him even further. Your grandfather and Bill . . . they, uh, found him wandering around, incoherent. He became very abusive when they tried to help him."

Michael immediately recalled Bill's sore arm, and he felt sick inside. Had Mickey hurt Bill? Had they fought?

"The two of them were unable to control him," Maggie continued, "so unfortunately they had to call Dr. Powell out at Bayview Sanitarium. They expected that holding him there overnight would be all that was needed."

"He's still there, isn't he?"

"Yes."

"Why?"

"He . . . hasn't come to grips with everything yet. He's having periods of extreme anger and depression. Dr. Powell recommended that he remain there until everyone felt sure Mickey was back in control."

"But I read that he was committed. That sounds terrible. Why did they have to do that?" Michael wanted to know.

"Because Mickey wouldn't stay there on his own. He kept insisting that he be released. The only way to keep him there was for the family to go through the procedure of having him declared incompetent."

"So everyone was against him."

"No, honey, we're all just trying to help," she said, her voice catching.

"How long is he going to have to stay in, then?"

"There's no way to know that right now, Michael. That's another reason why we haven't told you anything. There haven't been any definite answers to all the questions we knew you'd have."

"Have you seen him?" Michael asked after a pause.

"Of course. I go there every day. I've only actually talked to him a couple of times, but he's asked about you. I don't want you to ever think that he's forgotten about you. I know you've heard us say this over and over again, but you have to give him some time."

"When I finally get out of here, am I going to be able to see him?"

"I don't see why not. It will be up to Dr. Powell, but I would think that he'd approve. Mickey needs his family around him to help bring things back into focus."

"Maggie . . . is there anything else?"

"No," Maggie answered quickly, afraid that any hesitation on her part would be construed as more conspiracy. "I'm sure that by the time you're released, things will be more settled."

"Thanks. I knew I could count on you when the chips were down."

Maggie felt terrible. She loved the boy with all her heart, and was worried about what might happen to him and the friendship they shared when he discovered the complete truth. "I just want you to concentrate on getting well. We'll take care of everything else once you get out of there."

"Okay. I'll talk to you later."

"I'll be by tomorrow to see you."

"Bye." Michael hung up the phone and grimaced. Some of what Maggie had said just didn't ring true. He read the newspaper article again and promised himself that, as soon as he was out of the hospital, he would visit his father—come hell or high water!

Chapter Eight

Confession

"Ladies and gentlemen, this is your captain speaking," an authoritative voice said over the hum of the airplane's engines.

Kim looked up from her book and frowned as she checked her watch. The plane should have landed in Salem twenty minutes earlier.

"We have encountered some difficulty with the landing gear," the captain continued. "The electronic system has failed to lock in, and we've tried to manually release the gear without any success. I don't want to alarm you, but in the event that we are forced to land without assurances that all our systems are operating correctly, we will have to prepare for an emergency landing. The flight attendants will instruct you on the proper safety measures. Please remain calm, and thank you for your cooperation."

Kim's heart began to thud. Crash landing!

The plane became deathly quiet as every-

one on board listened to the instructions.
Kim shrank down in her seat. Her heart was
racing, but her mind was incredibly calm. *So
. . . this is it.* She looked out the window
and saw the city of Salem far below. *So
close, Doug. We were so close to finally
being back together.*

"Please, put your head down and hold
onto your ankles," a flight attendant insisted,
and Kim obeyed.

The tension in the plane was palpable as
the senior flight attendant tersely explained
the procedure. "A runway is being cleared
specifically for our landing. They will lay
down a bed of fire-retardant foam in case the
landing gear fails and we skid to a stop. The
success of this type of landing, when necessary, has been excellent. Please remain in
emergency position until we tell you otherwise.

A passenger near Kim asked, "When will
we know for sure?"

"Soon. The captain is continuing to circle
in order to burn as much fuel as possible. If
he can time it correctly, he can bring the
plane down with little or no fuel in the tanks,
and that will greatly reduce any possibility of
fire." The flight attendants buckled themselves
in, and the plane grew quiet.

"I love you Doug," Kim whispered, feeling
the plane start to descend. "I love you. . . ."

Doug paced up and down the concourse,
realizing that he had made a big mistake.
Bringing Hope with him to meet the plane

was turning out to be a disaster. The little girl had been running up and down between the rows of seats, playing hide-and-go-seek and peekaboo. Not only was he afraid he was going to lose her in the crowd, but he was worried that she was bothering everyone else in the airport.

"Ladies and gentlemen . . . Flight 167 from Chicago has encountered mechanical difficulties and has been delayed. If those of you waiting for this flight will proceed to our special briefing room, we will detail the problems and answer your questions at this time. Please follow our representative down the concourse."

Doug's heart nearly stopped beating. Flight 167? Kim's plane? He scooped Hope into his arms and followed the crowd, his footsteps accelerating with the pounding of his heart.

"Daddy . . . where's Kim? What's wrong?"

"I don't know, sweetheart. Let's go find out what the man has to say."

Once inside the airline's private room, he waited near the door, listening in horror to the explanation. ". . . there is a chance that the landing gear will function. We are proceeding with all the safety precautions because it is impossible for us to be certain that the gear will lock into position."

"Daddy, what's he saying? When are we going to see Kim?"

Doug kissed Hope's forehead and held her close. "I don't know yet, honey. Her plane is having some problems, and they're taking some steps to make sure it will be safe for it to land. We should know in a few minutes."

"I sure hope she's okay, Daddy. I like Kim. She's my friend."

"I know, princess. She's my friend too."

Kim, her head between her knees, felt the first jarring thud of impact as the plane hit the ground and bounced, before slamming into the runway a second time. The lights inside the plane went out. The horrifying scraping noises and the thud of the main fuselage smacking the ground were nearly deafening.

Sparks started flying everywhere. Several of the porthole windows popped out from the force of the impact. Foam came pouring in through the openings, partially filling the cabin. People started to scream.

"Oh, dear God," Kim prayed, her eyes squeezed tightly shut, her body braced as the plane shuddered, swerved off the pavement and finally came to rest in the marshy grass alongside the runway.

Kim lifted her head when she realized they'd stopped. They were alive. Wailing sirens filled the air.

The attendants were already snapping open the inflatable slides, wasting no time. "Come this way," the nearest one said, motioning, and Kim obliged.

She took off her heels and, holding them in one hand and her handbag in the other, slid down the rubber chute.

"Woooowww! Daddy, look at that! Is that the plane Kim is on?"

Doug's hands clutched the railing in front of the window, his grip tightening to the breaking point. Every muscle in his body was locked in tension. He'd left the briefing room and watched in horror as Kim's plane had landed. Now, passengers were actually sliding out of the emergency exits and making their way to waiting buses to be shuttled to the terminal.

"Is Kim okay?" Hope asked.

"She sure is! Come on."

He waited for more than half an hour before he found her in the baggage claim area. Small and fragile-looking, her face pale, her long, dark hair slightly rumpled, she was as beautiful as ever. And she was safe!

"Kim!" Doug's shout could have been heard anywhere in the complex. "Over here!"

She rushed toward him and collapsed in his arms. He nearly squeezed the breath out of her.

"Oh, Doug. I thought I'd never see you again." She covered his face with kisses and tried to stifle her tears.

"I missed you, too," he said.

"Me, too!" Hope looked up with round blue eyes.

"Oh, honey, I missed you! And I've never been so glad to see anyone in my life! I'm crazy about you." Kim brushed her tears away. "I brought you something from Chicago, but, unfortunately, it's in my suitcase, and who knows when I'll see that again."

Scooping Doug's daughter into her arms, Kim gave her a big kiss.

Doug wrapped his arm around Kim. He was touched by the obvious affection between Kim and his daughter. If only Hope could accept Julie as she had his ex-wife!

"A penny for your thoughts," Kim whispered.

"Not worth that much," he said with a wink. "Look, isn't that your bag?"

"One of them." Kim quickly tried to pick out her pieces of luggage, and Doug helped her, hoping he could drive all thoughts of Julie from his mind. But, as happy as he was that Kim was alive and with him now, he couldn't shake the memory of Julie . . . and her surprise decision to marry Don. Maybe he'd been a fool all along.

"Here we go!" Kim said. "That's the last of them, and look!" She unsnapped the largest bag and pulled out a stuffed koala bear. "For you, Hope. Even though I didn't go to Australia, I thought you'd like this."

"Oh!" Hope reached for the toy and her blue eyes sparkled. "You're the greatest, Kim."

"So are you, honey. And so's your dad!" She looked up at Doug with sparkling brown eyes, and Doug felt like an absolute heel. He'd only brought her back to get even with Julie—but now, after the plane crash, and watching her holding his child, he felt he owed her so much more.

Michael Horton threw his book down to the

foot of his bed. He'd been reading for several hours and was bored stiff. As far as he was concerned, it was time to get out of Brookville Hospital—and fast.

He thought about pushing his call button for the nurse, but he realized that he didn't need anything. At least, not anything she could help him with. Release papers. That's all he really needed.

Staring up at the sterile white ceiling, he muttered out loud, "What am I going to do?"

"About what?"

The lilting beauty of the voice, the concern that rang through each word, told him immediately who his surprise visitor was. He twisted on the bed and gazed into her innocent blue eyes. "Trish!"

"Hi, Michael. How are you?" Coming to the side of his bed, she leaned over and kissed him gently on the cheek. "Have you missed me?"

"More than you'll ever know! I'm so glad you're here."

"I would have come sooner if I could have."

"Oh, Trish." Michael just stared at her, overwhelmed. He loved Trish with all of his heart, but she just thought of him as a friend. "There's been so much going on that I feel like I'm totally in the dark."

"Are you talking about your dad?"

"Yeah. Is he okay? Do you know anything?"

Trish shook her head, and her long blond hair brushed her shoulders. "Only what I read in the newspaper, that he was committed to Bayview."

"I didn't even know *that* until a couple days ago. My family is keeping everything a big secret because . . . God, I don't even really know why. They keep giving me some story about my not being up to it. Maggie tried to tell me that they're protecting me."

"And you don't believe her?"

"I don't know what to believe! I had to sneak an old newspaper from the lounge—otherwise I still wouldn't know anything. Then I called Maggie and got her to fill me in." His eyes darkened. "But she's still holding something back. I can feel it. Oh, Trish, I gotta get out of here and go visit Dad!"

With a sparkle in her eye, she winked and said, "That shouldn't be long. You're looking pretty good to me. When *do* you get out?"

"You tell me. The doctor keeps saying any day. Bill's probably paying him to keep me here!"

"You don't really think so?"

"I don't know," he muttered. Then, noticing her shift her weight from one foot to the other, he said, "Hey, c'mon. You don't have to just stand there. Pull one of those chairs over and sit down." He grinned from ear to ear. "You're not leaving here for a long time."

"You're right about that. The apartment is a real bore without you."

"Really?"

"What do you think?" She gave him a shy smile. "I . . . I was hoping that you might want to come back to our apartment when you get out. Okay?"

His heart skipped a beat. Just looking at her did strange, wonderful things to him. "I haven't even thought that far ahead. I've been so anxious to get out and see Dad that I've barely considered where I was going to live."

"So you want to go back to the farm?"

"Not really." He blushed a little. "I missed living with you."

"Good!"

Trish was about to give a convincing argument in favor of his return, but just then the door opened and Maggie walked in. She stopped short when she noticed the pretty young girl at Michael's bedside.

"Maggie!" he exclaimed.

"Hello, Michael. I'm not interrupting, am I?"

"No, come on in." Michael raised the bed and scooted himself up higher. "You remember me talking about my, er, roommate? Well, this is her. Maggie, this is Trish Clayton. Trish, this is my father's wife, Maggie."

Maggie beamed. "So you're 'the girl he left behind'?"

"Maggie!" Blushing, Michael tried to intervene.

Maggie chuckled, ignoring him. "Well, it's a real pleasure to meet you, Trish. Michael and I had many a talk out at the farm about you."

"He only said good things, I hope. It's nice meeting you, Mrs. Horton."

"Please . . . call me Maggie."

"Maggie it is."

Maggie stepped closer to the bed and turned

to Michael. "I thought I'd better come see how you were doing after our phone call."

"I'm okay."

She glanced at the girl. "Does Trish know what's going on?"

"Yeah. Sure. Trish and I were just talking about it. All I want is to get out of here and go see Dad myself. Then everything will be better."

"You have to understand why I hid the facts from you. It wasn't because—"

"Hey, don't sweat it. I know you were doing what you thought was best. And if Mom and Grandpa and Bill and everyone were working on you, you really didn't have a choice. I don't blame you. I'm just glad you finally talked to me. I needed to know."

Trish took hold of Michael's hand. "I'll see you a little later. Maggie can have my seat while I take a walk."

"You just got here," Michael protested, and then, seeing a movement, turned to the doorway. His jaw dropped when he met his mother's worried eyes. "I can't believe it. Ten minutes ago I was bored out of my skull, and now I should be selling admission tickets."

"Hi," she said cautiously. "How are you feeling?"

"I'm okay," he said, his voice cold.

"And you, Maggie? How are you holding up?"

"As well as can be expected."

Trish looked uncomfortable. Michael grabbed her hand and squeezed it. "Mom, this is Trish Clayton."

"Oh—the friend you shared an apartment with," Laura said. "Nice to meet you."

"Share. As in present tense," Michael said firmly.

As Laura stepped to the side of the bed, she saw the censure in her son's eyes and felt the tension in the small room. "Is something wrong?"

Maggie licked her lips nervously. "I think you should know that Michael and I have had a talk about Mickey."

Laura blanched. "Oh! What about?" she asked calmly, though she was shaking inwardly. Maggie wouldn't have told Michael about Bill! She couldn't have!

"I've explained that Mickey is in Bayview to get psychiatric help, and that the family had to commit him because he was unwilling to stay there on his own."

"But why did you say anything? I thought we'd agreed—"

"Because of this, Mom!" Michael snatched up the newspaper and tossed it onto the floor. "You could have told me, you know! I'm not a baby!"

Laura glanced toward Trish, and then back at Michael.

"Look, it's okay," Michael said defensively. "Trish knows everything that I do—and I don't hide things from her, anyway."

"We weren't trying to hide anything from you—"

"Was this Bill's idea?" Michael demanded, furious.

"No. We all agreed to tell you when you

were completely well, Mike. Your accident was pretty serious, and above all else, we just wanted you to get better."

Michael glared at his mother. "No more secrets?" he asked.

Swallowing hard, Laura whispered, "No more." She felt guilty all over again. She glanced at Maggie, but Mickey's wife was pretending interest in the book Michael had discarded.

"Okay, so now that I'm better, when can I get out of here? Dr. Chamberlain never gives me a straight answer. Have you talked to him?"

"Yes. Just before I came in. And believe it or not, I can spring you the day after tomorrow!"

"All right!" Michael beamed and fell back on his pillows. "That's fantastic!"

"According to the doctor, your ribs are mending and your blood count is normal. So, he intends to take out your stitches tomorrow, and then you'll be free as a bird."

"About time!"

"That's terrific," Trish added, just as Dr. Chamberlain came into the room.

"So, you already got the good news that I'm kicking you out of here?" he said genially.

"Believe me, I'm ready!"

"Okay, but just because you're getting out, that doesn't mean you can start playing football or anything. You're going to have to spend most of your time resting in bed for a while. But you can do that at home as well as here, so you might as well be released. As long as you promise to take it easy."

"I promise." But a frown suddenly crossed Michael's face as he looked around the room at his visitors and wondered where he'd end up.

He'd been at the farm living with Maggie and Mickey when the accident had occurred. Laura wanted him to return to live with her and Bill. Trish wanted him to come back to their apartment.

Where was home?

Chapter Nine
The Plan

It had taken a while, but Doug finally finished loading Kim's luggage into the car. "All set," he said as he slammed the trunk and climbed into the driver's seat.

"It's good to be back," Kim admitted, her arms wrapped securely around Hope as Doug drove away from the terminal. Overhead, huge planes were taking off and arriving as if nothing out of the ordinary had occurred. "And it's good to be on level ground again."

Doug saw Kim smiling at him, and he hated himself. Though she'd used him often in the past, he didn't like turning the tables on her—not even for Julie. He scowled as he wove through the heavy rush-hour traffic.

Kim placed her hand on his knee. "Would it be all right if we stopped at Don Craig's office?"

He glanced at her. Though he'd like nothing better than to parade Kim in front of Don, his conscience twinged. "He might not be there."

"I know, but I have to settle with him for the work he did for me." Kim's voice was tired. The last person she wanted to face was that holier-than-thou attorney, but she had to square her account with Don and now that she was back in Salem, the sooner it was done, the better.

"It's late—"

"Come on. Surely someone's still at his office."

"He's not your biggest fan, you know."

"Neither were you," she reminded him.

"It's your funeral," he said, taking the freeway exit leading toward downtown. "But if it's what you want, let's hope we can still catch him there."

Though he couldn't have planned Kim's return to Salem better himself, Doug was nervous. What if the plan backfired? What if Kim found out he was using her?

"Aren't you coming up?" she asked when they were parked in front of the law office.

"Do you want me to?"

"Of course, silly! You, too, Hope." She grabbed the little girl's hand and helped her up the concrete steps, through the foyer and into the elevator.

The receptionist was just locking up. "Oh, Mrs. Douglas," she said. "I'm afraid we're closing."

"I just wanted to settle my bill," Kim said.

Shrugging, the woman stepped aside and

let them in, just as Don walked out of his
office, shrugging into his coat. "I'll be in court
in the morning. Don't expect me until
afternoon—" He stopped short. His eyes
locked with Doug's.

Kim gave him one of her breathtaking
smiles. "Hi, Don."

"Kim, this is a surprise."

"I thought I'd better settle my bill with you
and thank you for helping me try to claim
my inheritance."

"No problem at all," Don said, perplexed.
What the hell was Kim up to? He saw the
way Doug's arm was draped around Kim's
shoulders, and felt uneasy. Something wasn't
right. "Did you need to see me?"

"No," she said brightly. "As I said, just
paying up." She felt good about being on the
ground in one piece and was thrilled that
Doug was being so attentive. Not even Don's
perplexed expression could ruin her good
mood.

Hope ran over to the couch and plopped
down. "Daddy, I'm tired. When can we go
home with Kim?"

"Just a minute, princess. We have to take
care of a little business first. Then we can all
go home together." Doug watched Don carefully for a reaction, but the attorney's expression didn't change.

"You really didn't need to come in," Don
said, glancing at Doug. "I was going to drop
you a bill in the mail."

"I'd rather just take care of it now. I won't
be needing your services anymore, so I'd like

to wipe the slate clean," Kim answered.

"Has there been an invoice typed for Mrs. Douglas?" Don asked the receptionist.

The girl looked nervously at her boss. "Bonnie didn't give me one. Is there something I can do?"

Don's smile tightened. "No, I'll handle it. Why don't you go on home? I'll lock up." Wishing he could just get rid of Kim, Doug and Hope, Don walked over to the bookkeeper's desk. Fumbling through her files, he tried to find the statement for Kim so he could get her out of the office. "Here, I think this is it. Yes . . . this should do it for everything," he said, handing her the rough draft of a bill for his services. "I'll send you a typed invoice and receipt later."

With a flourish, Doug grabbed the invoice. "Let me get this, Kim. I'm going to do everything I can to take care of you from now on."

Kim was taken aback. She looked at Doug as if he'd gone crazy. "You don't have to do that."

"I know. I want to."

Don's eyes narrowed. Doug Williams was up to something. He could feel it.

With a lopsided grin, Doug handed Don a check. "There you go. That should cover everything. Thanks a lot." Then, clasping an arm around Kim's waist, he said, "Let's hope we don't ever go through any of this again."

"Er . . . right," Kim agreed.

"Let's go!" Hope demanded, walking to the door.

"We will, honey." Doug kissed Kim on the

cheek, then smiled at Don. "I guess I should thank you for everything you've done."

"No thanks necessary."

"But you really helped Kim. Not to mention me. And Julie. Even when you obviously didn't want to."

"What's this all about, Williams?" Don demanded, leaning one hip on the corner of the receptionist's desk.

Doug's blue eyes glinted. "Well, Don, whether you know it or not, you've done Kim and me a big favor. You've opened Julie's eyes to our problems, and by so doing, you've opened mine. After talking to Julie the other morning, I realized that Kim will always be special to me, and that we deserve a second chance."

Kim could barely believe her ears or her good luck, and she snuggled closer into his encircling arm. Smiling down at her, Doug called for Hope. "C'mon, ladies. It's time to go home and let Mr. Craig be on his way. Thanks again, Don."

"Don't mention it," the attorney replied mechanically. When the door closed, Don didn't move. "What the hell was that all about?" he muttered. Obviously, Kim had been as surprised as Don when Doug had announced that they were back together.

It just didn't wash. Thinking back to the night Doug had returned from Chicago, all he could picture was a man who was hopelessly in love with Julie, relentless in his attempts to steal her away from Don. Doug was now doing a complete about-face.

Doug Williams wouldn't turn his back on Julie that quickly. What Don had just witnessed had to be the charade of the year.

Still frowning, Don dropped into the receptionist's chair and reached for the phone. His fingers drummed impatiently as he waited.

"Hello?"

"Hi, gorgeous."

"Don," she murmured, and he could envision Julie's blue eyes dancing. "Where are you? Aren't you coming over?"

"Oh, yeah. I'll be there shortly. I was delayed here at the office by a very unusual couple."

"Unusual? Now, Don, don't tell me anything kinky," she said, laughing.

"Kinkier than you can imagine. Guess who's back together?"

"Listen, I don't even know who's apart."

"Would you believe Doug and Kim?"

He heard her gasp, and wanted to kick himself for killing her laughter and high spirits.

"What?" she whispered.

"That's right. Doug just brought Kim in here and paid her legal bill. Made a big deal about how they were back together again. Hope was even with them, and they made it known that they were one big, happy family now." Don hated himself for what he was doing, but he just couldn't stop. Julie meant everything to him, and he had to be sure that she was over Doug for good.

"Is that right?" she said, her voice toneless.

"Hey, I didn't mean to upset you," he

apologized, feeling like a jerk. "You told me that you two had officially broken everything off the other day. I thought you'd be glad that he's not moping around or planning something stupid to spite you."

"Obviously he isn't," she said in a low voice.

Don could almost hear the tears in her voice. "You always thought there was something going on between them, didn't you?"

"Just forget it, Don," Julie said quietly. "It's not important to me. What Doug Williams does with his life is his business."

"You're right. I just called to let you know why I was running late. I'll see you in a little while, okay?"

"Okay," she murmured, and then she hung up.

Don grabbed his briefcase, then paused. He realized that he'd been had—by one of the best con artists around. Doug had always had a way of manipulating people, and Don felt as if he'd just fallen into a neatly set trap. "Smooth move," he muttered, snapping off the lights. "Real smooth."

Maggie sat at the table in the kitchen of her Brookville farm and stared out the window. Gray skies and a persistent drizzle of cold rain made the rolling acres seem forlorn and lifeless. The scenery here was as dreary as her view from the tiny apartment near the sanitarium.

Someone had to take care of the farm, she thought wearily.

From her vantage point in the kitchen, she could see the hay wagon still propped on a jack near the barn. She noticed the chipped paint on the outbuildings, the rusted downspouts and the eerie feeling of neglect that hung like a shadow over the farm.

She'd spent most of the morning trying to put the farm accounts back into some kind of order, and was now thoroughly depressed. Standing, she stretched and was making a fresh pot of tea when the phone rang.

"Mrs. Horton? This is Jan at Valley National Bank."

"Hi," Maggie said, cradling the phone between shoulder and ear as she refilled the teapot. "What's up?"

"Well, I hate to bother you, but I've got a problem with your account."

"Oh?"

"I'm afraid we're showing an overdraft."

Maggie set the teapot on the counter with a bang. "You're kidding."

"I'm afraid not. I double-checked our figures, because I know this has never happened before. I'm sure it's just a simple mistake somewhere. Maybe you could come down, and we can go over your statement?"

"Sounds like I'd better," Maggie replied, eyeing the clock.

"Great."

"I'll be there a little after eleven, if that's okay with you."

"Fine. Thanks, Maggie."

"Thanks for calling me, Jan. I'll try to

straighten this out from my end right now."

"Bye."

Maggie grabbed her checkbook and added the figures again. Everything worked. "The bank's wrong," she said, chewing on the end of her pencil as her eyes scanned the ledgers. Then she saw it. A simple mistake—simple, but large—of two thousand dollars, where she'd added in the same deposit twice. "Oh, no," she whispered, realizing that the overdraft at the bank was the first of a long string of checks that wouldn't be covered.

"What am I going to do?" she wondered aloud, feeling despair wash over her. The farm was falling down around her, most of the equipment needed to be repaired, feed supplies were low and she missed Mickey with all of her heart. If only he were here! If only things could be as they had been before his memory had returned!

Her throat clogged and tears burned in her eyes, but she wouldn't let herself break down. Instead, she walked to the kitchen sink and ran cold water from the tap. Sluicing the near-freezing liquid over her face, she grabbed a towel and patted herself dry.

"That's enough of that!" she muttered, and grabbed her coat. Tossing it over her shoulders, she opened the door and ran through the downpour to the pickup. The old engine coughed and whined but eventually turned over, and Maggie headed into town.

Twenty minutes later, she pulled into a space in the bank's parking lot. Dashing through puddles on the asphalt, she hurried into the bank and brushed the rain from her face as she approached Jan Marshall's desk.

"Maggie, it's so good to see you. You haven't been in for quite a while. How're things going?"

"Obviously, not too well." Maggie forced a smile. "At least, bouncing checks isn't my idea of smooth sailing."

"It happens to the best of us."

"Not to me," Maggie said firmly as she took a seat and balanced her purse on her lap.

"So, tell me, how's Marty—I mean, Mickey—doing?"

Maggie's brown eyes clouded. "It's hard to say. Sometimes he seems just fine . . . other times I don't even recognize him."

"I'm sure he's going to snap out of it anytime now. Can I get you a cup of coffee?"

"Yes, thanks."

After sipping from the Styrofoam cup, Maggie set it down and pulled out her checkbook. "I've gone over my records, and I hate to admit it, but I've found a mistake—a doozy."

"Perfectly understandable, given your circumstances."

"There's no excuse," Maggie said. "I just haven't been paying close enough attention to business, and that's not right. We have some money in our savings account that I'm going to have to transfer to checking for now."

Jan made a note and filled out the proper

withdrawal slip, which Maggie signed. "I'm so sorry I had to call you, Maggie."

"No, it was my fault. Everything is going to be okay. We have an installment payment coming on our wheat contracts next week. That will be more than enough money to see me through until March."

"Good! So who's running the farm— besides you?"

Maggie's stiff shoulders slumped a little. "I've only got one hired hand left. If Mickey isn't home by the end of this month, I'm just going to have to hire someone else on, too . . . like before."

"I hope it doesn't come to that."

"Well, I've been there before; I can do it again. I'll find a good foreman and get things running at full speed. There's no reason why that farm can't support us." -

Jan nodded. "If there's anything we can do for you, Maggie, please don't hesitate to call. You've been a good and faithful customer to the bank, and we'll be here for you if you need us."

"Thanks, Jan. It means a lot to me to hear you say that. Let's just hope that everything goes smoothly and we won't need to meet like this again."

"Amen."

"I'll talk to you later."

"Bye."

Maggie left the bank and turned up her collar against the cold wind and rain as she hurried to the pickup. The next step was to talk to Mrs. Ferguson and give up the apartment near Bayview. Maybe, with a little luck, she could get some of her rent back.

"Sure, and maybe the pope isn't Catholic," she muttered, grinding the gearshift into reverse. If only she could hold everything together until Mickey was well and home again!

Mickey stared blankly out the window of his room. He could see the bare limbs of the trees in the distance, the black branches silhouetted against the gray sky. Rain pelted the glass and drizzled down the panes. It was a classically depressing day.

But Mickey wasn't going to let the weather get him down. Not today. He knew that it was nearly time for a visit from Dr. Powell, and he looked forward to the confrontation and the games he would play with the good doctor.

Though Laura had yet to be assigned to his case, he was sure it would happen—and soon. Right on schedule, the door clanged open, and Mickey smiled to himself.

"Hello, Mickey. How are you today?"

"It's hard to say, Doc. I've been looking out the window and wondering if I'm ever going to be a free man again."

"Of course you will be! Why would you think that you wouldn't?"

"Don't I have to be well before you release me from here?"

"Yes."

"And that's probably impossible. Right?"

"Of course not."

Mickey ran his fingers along the cool glass pane and sighed. "I can't picture myself getting over even the first hurdle if I can't get past dealing with Laura," he said with a frown.

"Did someone say that you wouldn't have the opportunity to deal with Laura?"

"Not in so many words. But it's obvious that you've dismissed the idea of her being my counselor."

"That's not entirely true."

Rubbing the kinks from his neck, Mickey began to pace. "I need her to unlock all the secrets of my past, you know. That way I can deal with the present."

"Maybe if you'd try to talk to someone else first, you could change my mind about Laura."

"Come on, Doc. You're playing me. You know I don't feel comfortable talking to anyone else."

Dr. Powell studied the large man. Mickey was clever, and he had to be careful. "What about what Laura wants? What if she doesn't want to work with you? Or what if she thinks she can't help?"

Mickey's back went rigid. "Let me talk to her. Let me hear her say that."

"I don't know if I can."

"You won't even let it go that far!"

"You really don't trust me, do you?" Dr. Powell asked.

"I guess I need some proof."

"Would you believe me if I told you that Laura and Bill are on their way out here right now to talk to you?"

Mickey stopped dead in his tracks and stared straight at the doctor. "Are you telling me the truth?"

"I've told Laura everything you've said to me. I've outlined the pros and cons of her involvement. I've left the decision up to her. Bill, of course, has had his input, as well as the rest of your family, I'm sure. But the decision is going to be Laura's. I don't know what that choice is going to be, but they called to tell me that they both wanted to come and see you today."

Mickey walked to his bed and eased himself down on the hard mattress. He had to work at suppressing a smile. *Laura is mine at last!* "Am I going to be able to see her alone?"

"Not today. Bill will be with her, and I'll be in the room, too."

"Everybody checking me out just to see how crazy I am when I'm with her?" Mickey surmised.

"After your run-in with Linda Phillips, I want to find out what triggers your violent tendencies before I leave you alone with *anyone.*"

"I guess that's fair, Doc. Thanks for warning me. I'll be on my best behavior."

"I don't want you on any kind of behavior. I want you to be yourself. Just relax, and say what's on your mind. That isn't so difficult, is it?"

"No, not at all." Mickey shifted restlessly on the bed. "I thought I'd been doing that for you. I've told you I want Laura as my counselor. I've told you that I don't want to see anyone else until I talk to her. I don't see how I could be more open and honest."

"Well, it looks like you're going to get your opportunity. But tell me—if things don't go well with Laura, what are you going to do?"

"Things will go just fine, Doc. She'll understand me and want to help," Mickey said, stretching and trying to hold back his laughter. How stupid they all were—so easily manipulated!

"How can you be so sure?"

"Hey, we go way back. There's more than just a passing acquaintance here," he said mockingly. "Besides, she owes me. She owes me big!"

Dr. Powell tried to goad him on. "You think that after what you've done, anyone owes you anything?"

"You better believe it, Doc." Rising from the bed, Mickey resumed his pacing, alternately glancing at Powell and the dark sky beyond the window. "My wife and my brother both owe me." Catching himself, he stopped his tirade and sighed.

"Whether they owe you anything or not, we'll monitor the meeting today, and then all sit back and evaluate what will be best. So don't get your hopes up. This is just one more step in the process."

"At least it gives me my chance to talk to Laura."

"I'll be back later, Mickey. Get some rest."

"Thanks, Doc."

"You needn't thank me. It was their deci-

sion to come out here and see you. I just
hope it works out well for everyone concerned."

"It will!" Mickey watched the door shut,
and then allowed himself the luxury of a
grin. So, big brother and his darling little
wifey had finally felt guilty enough to show
up together! Mickey could hardly wait.

The wipers slapped aside the rain as the car
sped along the winding road to Bayview.

"What's on your mind?" Bill asked, trying
to draw Laura out of her silence. They had
covered half the distance between Salem and
Bayview, and Bill wanted to talk to his wife
before it was too late.

"Not much," she said, looking out the window at the passing countryside. Pine and
oak trees knifed upward toward the gray,
overcast sky.

"You expect me to believe that?"

Smiling, Laura reached over and rested
her hand on his shoulder. "I guess not. I'm
thinking about Mickey."

"I knew that," he said, his fingers tightening on the steering wheel. "What about
him?"

"I was remembering some of the good
times when we were first married and
Michael was born. I really thought that everything was going to be all right back then."

Bill's lips thinned. "I remember going crazy
with jealousy about that time. I wanted you
so badly for my own wife."

"I guess I've always known that someday

we'd have to pay for our mistakes. I have the feeling that today is just going to be the beginning," she said soberly.

"Maybe," Bill said, placing his arm around her shoulders. "It won't be easy, I know. But I'll be there with you. I want you to let me explain to him what happened—how Michael was conceived. It was my fault, and I should be the one he hears it from."

"My knight in shining armor," she teased, glancing up at his handsome profile and seeing the hard set of his jaw.

"Unfortunately, not all the time."

"Do you think it matters now who says what?" she asked, ignoring the knots twisting her stomach.

"Who knows? What I do know is that now we have each other, and Michael—and now a beautiful daughter. We have to keep our family as our number-one priority. We'll do everything we can for Mickey up to a point. I'm ready to bare my soul today to try to help him. But I'm not going to sacrifice my family for him. I can only go so far. And I don't want you to take on the weight of the world, either. Understand?"

"Yes." She leaned back and felt the comfort of his arm around her shoulders.

"Right now, I can tell you, I don't trust my brother at all. Unstable or not—who knows? But I remember looking into his eyes that night, with that gun staring me in the face . . . it's going to take me a while to forget that."

She shivered. "Me, too."

"So, Dr. Horton, don't be fooled by anything today. Listen and observe. But the man you're going to see is really a stranger."

"I know," she said, sighing. "But, remember, this is my job. I see emotionally disturbed people all the time, and I know what chameleons they can be. I'm not going to make a judgment based on one meeting. I'm only going to try to see if it's even remotely possible for me to help him. I thought we agreed that we'd at least try."

"It's just that I love you so much," Bill admitted, his voice rough with emotion. "And you've been through so much already."

"I can handle it," she whispered, snuggling closer to him. "As long as you're with me."

"I always will be."

"Good." She kissed him on the cheek and forced a trembling smile, just as they rounded the final bend. Ahead, perched high on the hill behind a tall wire fence, stood Bayview Sanitarium. Laura shuddered. "Let's just pray that everything goes well."

As the gates to Bayview loomed ahead, Bill began to sweat. His jaw set and his eyes shadowed, he whispered, "God, I hope there's something we can do for him—and that no one gets hurt. For his sake, for yours and for mine, I'm praying for a miracle."

Laura grabbed his arm and hugged it tightly. "So am I, honey. So am I."

Chapter Ten

The Prisoner of Love

Laura could hardly believe that the large man staring blankly out the window of his room was Mickey. He'd aged since she'd last seen him, and his eyes looked almost dead.

"Mickey?" Laura said quietly as Dr. Powell locked the door behind Bill.

Mickey didn't move, and Bill edged closer to Laura. The look on Mickey's face made his skin crawl.

"Let me handle this," Dr. Powell suggested in a low voice. He walked to Mickey's side and touched his shoulder. "Mickey. You have some visitors. Bill and Laura are here."

Mickey wanted to laugh out loud. So they'd fallen into his trap! He turned around slowly, his eyes revealing nothing.

"Hello, Mickey," Laura said. "It's good to see you."

One of his brows arched. "If it isn't good old brother Bill and his bride," he said, and then, hearing the taunt in his own voice, dredged up a cold smile and looked straight at Laura. "Glad you could still find some time for your ex."

"I just want to help," Laura said.

Bill eyed his brother warily. "What's this all about, Mick? I want to know exactly why you've insisted on working with Laura."

"Let's all stay calm," Dr. Powell suggested, pulling up a chair. "Why don't we try to find enough seats for everyone and relax? I'm sure there's a lot to talk about, and we don't have that much time."

Mickey leaned against the wall and watched Laura as she sat uneasily on the foot of his bed. *Just where she belongs.* He folded his arms over his chest. "Okay. I'll start. How's little Jennifer doing?"

Laura glanced at Bill. "She's wonderful," she said.

"I'll bet."

Bill sat down next to his wife. "She's doing great, Mickey. When you get out of here you have to see her. She's beautiful."

"Like her mother." Mickey slid a glance at Laura.

"Right. Like her mother," Bill agreed.

"So, how are things with you?" Laura asked.

"Can't complain."

"That's not the Mickey Horton I knew," she said, her eyes locking with his. If only she could read something, anything, on his face.

"The Mickey Horton you knew has been

gone for a long time. I guess all that work out on the farm has changed me."

Laura smiled, feeling she was making headway. "I've gotten to know Maggie pretty well. We see each other when we're visiting Michael. She's a good woman, and she loves you very much."

Mickey's eyes narrowed. "So it seems."

"Have you heard that Michael is getting out of the hospital tomorrow?"

"Maggie said something about it. But let's cut the small talk, okay?"

"Okay." Laura squared her shoulders and met his gaze. "We need to talk to you about getting you out of here. Dr. Powell has told us that you won't consider therapy sessions with anyone but me. Why?"

"Because no one knows me as well as you do."

"It's that simple?" Bill asked doubtfully.

"That simple."

Laura wasn't sure. "Couldn't you talk to someone else first, before I work with you?"

"I'm not comfortable discussing my problems with anyone else. They're personal. I think you can understand why."

To her annoyance, she blushed. "Okay. But do you think you can deal with me as a psychiatrist, and not as your ex-wife?"

"Yes." His gaze was even, his face emotionless. "But I won't forget you were my wife. I can't."

Bill linked his fingers together. "Before we go any further, Mickey, you've got to let me explain a few things."

"Sure, why not?"

"I think I should explain what happened, years ago . . . between Laura and me."

"I think I've already got that figured out, Bill."

"No . . . no, you don't, Mick. And it's something that maybe I should have told you a long time ago."

"Why?" Mickey said coldly. "If it hadn't been for this freak accident with the hay wagon, I never would have known. I'd have lived my whole life in ignorance, and you two would have pulled it off, slick as a whistle."

"We've never been trying to pull anything off," Bill said heavily. "We did what we thought was best for everyone—"

"Oh, yeah. I think having an affair with your brother's wife is usually the best for everyone. Especially your brother!"

"It wasn't like that."

Mickey's eyes gleamed. "Don't tell me there's been another immaculate conception?"

Bill's fists tightened. "Listen. I loved Laura long before you even knew up from sideways."

"Territorial rights? First claim? Is that what you're trying to tell me?"

"How do you think I felt when Laura broke off our engagement?"

"Seems to me it was the other way around, but I don't know. And I really don't care."

"Well, I'm going to tell you," Bill said, his

eyes narrowed on his brother. "I'm going to tell you everything whether you care or not."

This should be good, Mickey thought, but feigned indifference. "Spare me the details."

"Just listen to him," Laura insisted.

Bill rose and faced his brother. "Laura is the only woman I've ever loved. When I lost her, it was like the end of my life. I had nothing I wanted to live for."

"You found a way past that I see."

"I was literally going out of my mind," Bill admitted quietly.

"Kind of like I am now, huh?"

Ignoring his brother's taunt, Bill continued, "It was shortly after I got back from California and found out that you two had gotten married that I snapped. I was working with Laura in the hospital day after day. Having her so close, loving her so much . . . it became more than I could bear. We were working late one night, and I . . . I took her to my office." He closed his eyes at the memory, revolted at what he'd done.

"Go on."

"I knew no one else was around," Bill said softly. "I grabbed her and pushed her onto the sofa."

"Oh, God," Laura whispered.

Mickey's face drained of color, and Laura looked as if she wanted to fall through the floor. Tears filled her eyes, and she couldn't look at Mickey.

"Look, I don't think I want to hear this—"

"She fought me, Mickey," Bill said, his voice trembling. "She kicked and hit and pushed . . . but it was no use. I was so much stronger. I raped her, Mickey." Bill's voice cracked. "And I've had to live with that."

Mickey's fists balled and he looked at Laura. Tears were tracking down her cheeks. "You bastard!" he ground out, staring at his brother in disbelief.

"Laura loved you, Mickey. She wanted your marriage to work. That's why she didn't say anything to anyone. She didn't want our family destroyed. She knew how it would crush you and Dad and Mom. She swore she wouldn't ever tell, as long as I promised that I would never try anything like that again."

"A hard promise to make, huh, brother? And an even harder one to keep!"

Bill's eyes flashed. "I kept it, Mickey. It was hell, but I never touched her again. Laura was never once unfaithful to you all the while you were married."

"It's true," Laura whispered, her throat swollen.

Mickey stared at her. "God, this is sick! You ended up marrying a man who *raped* you? That's what you expect me to believe? Laura Horton, a woman who knew her own mind, a psychiatrist, for God's sake, married a man who raped her?"

"Yes!"

"Give me some credit," Mickey said. "I'm not crazy enough to believe that one."

"Then think what you like," Laura said, rising to stand near Bill. "But the truth is that after . . . after . . ."

"The rape," Mickey supplied, his face ashen.

"Yes . . . I was hurt and confused. I didn't know what to do. I was angry. I hated him. I wanted to run to you and cry and tell you about it and swear that I loved you. But I couldn't. I knew that it would destroy your relationship with Bill. I knew that your dad and mom would be devastated. I'm sorry, Mickey. I had to keep the secret."

"What a great performance," Mickey said, clapping. "Good job, Laura. You would have made a very convincing actress."

"Knock it off, Mick."

"And you, if it's true, I should knock your block off!" he said, turning on his brother. "Tell me something, Bill. How did dear old Dad get involved in this? How come he knew and I didn't?"

Laura blinked back her tears. "Remember how much we wanted children and couldn't conceive?"

"Oh, God, no—"

"We both went in for fertility tests. On the day I went to tell him I was pregnant, Tom had your results showing that you were sterile."

"This gets better and better," Mickey muttered, but slumped onto the bed.

"Your father asked me how it was possible. I broke down and told him everything. He agreed with me that it would be best if we didn't tell either you or Bill about the results of the tests. You both would naturally assume that you were the father. And I had to keep the baby—I couldn't even consider abortion," she whispered, remembering those agonizing months. "Can't you see, Mickey? That baby was going to be the only child I would ever have!"

"Because I'm sterile."

"Yes!"

Mickey ran a shaking hand over his chin. "Then how did Bill ever find out?"

"Tommy—"

"All my brothers knew about it?" Mickey gasped.

"No. Tommy's wife found out and told me," Bill admitted.

Mickey's eyes glittered dangerously. "You mean Kitty . . . the woman that you wound up in jail for killing. Excuse me—manslaughter, wasn't it?"

Bill nodded, his lips taut. "That's right. Kitty had obtained the test results and was threatening to go to the family and tell them everything. I grabbed her as she was about to run out and, during the struggle when I tried to stop her and talk some sense into her, she died of a heart attack."

"Six months in jail if I recall correctly," Mickey said, replaying in his mind the courtroom scene in which he'd defended Bill.

"Of course, it wasn't Bill's fault—" Laura began.

"Of course not," Mickey said mockingly.

Bill's eyes turned cold. "But through it all, the secret of Michael's parentage became a bigger and bigger issue. We feared that the truth would destroy the family."

"Instead of just destroying me."

"We didn't intend to hurt you," Laura said.

"Do you really expect me to believe that there was nothing between you and Laura ever again?"

"That's right."

Mickey looked from Laura to Bill and back again. Damned if they didn't look like innocent lambs. After all their lies, and their betrayal. His face hardened as memories played through his mind. "I can remember all the times I walked into rooms and found the two of you alone . . . and *I* felt like the outsider. I could feel that something had been going on behind my back."

"Nothing ever did, Mickey." Bill's voice had a hard edge to it. "Not that *I* didn't want something to happen. But Laura wouldn't have anything to do with me. She finally admitted that she still loved me, but that was the end of it. She wanted to make her life with you and Michael work."

Laura inched her chin upward. "I loved you when I married you, Mickey. I loved you right up till the time you started cheating on me because you didn't trust me. I never would have left you. I guess it just wasn't meant to be. Don't ask me how it's possible to love two men . . . but I did. Maybe it's because you're brothers, I don't know. But one thing you must believe—I never cheated on you, and I never wanted to hurt you."

"This is too much—"

"Maybe it is," Dr. Powell interjected quietly. "Maybe this is enough for right now.

What do you say, Mickey?"

But Mickey had withdrawn. He couldn't hear anything save the voices in his mind, little demons that kept pricking his brain, telling him that Bill and Laura were lying to him again, just as they had in the past. Once more they were laughing at him, and they were going to pay—with their lives!

"Mickey?" Dr. Powell gave up. "He's gone again. This happens sometimes. He'll be back."

"Maybe it's just his way of dealing with pain," Laura said, feeling a wave of guilt wash over her.

"We'll leave him for now. Give him a little time alone. Maybe later we can see him again," Dr. Powell said.

"Today?"

"We'll see."

"I'd like that," Laura said. "I have to help him."

"I don't know if it's possible," Bill muttered, looking at the supine form on the hard mattress. Mickey stared straight up at the ceiling, obviously not hearing anything.

"I've got to try! No matter what, I'm going to help him," Laura vowed as Dr. Powell locked the door behind them.

Perfect, Mickey thought. *Laura the whore and Bill the rapist, I'm going to kill you both*.

In the hallway, Laura followed Dr. Powell back to his office while Bill placed a call to University Hospital to check on several of his patients.

"Well, what do you think? How did he take all that?" she asked Dr. Powell.

"Calmer than I expected," he said, lighting his pipe. "He was obviously angered and almost lost it a few times, but I would have to say that his reactions were normal, except at the very end."

"Yes, that was my impression, too. Mickey seemed perfectly normal . . . given the circumstances."

"You'd have a difficult time convincing a stranger that he wasn't a hundred percent. Still, he has these rages . . . he obviously needs help."

"And I want to give it to him."

"Are you sure?"

"Dr. Powell, you saw him in there. Wouldn't you say that part of his problem is that he hasn't given me up? That he still loves me?"

"That seemed pretty apparent."

"Well, then, I think I have to work with him so he can understand how *I* feel. I still love him—as a brother-in-law. But I love the life I have with Bill and my new baby. Mickey has to learn that he can still love me, but he has to go on with his life from here."

"I agree."

"I think I should go back and talk to Mickey for a minute, tell him that I will work with him, if that's what he still wants. And I think I should see him alone."

"Do you think that's wise?"

"Yes. I have to establish a pattern of mutual trust with him as soon as possible."

Powell drew on his pipe. "Well, he wasn't the least bit violent with you," he mused.

"He wouldn't be. We care about each other."

"Okay. Whenever you're ready. Oh, there is one more thing. While you're handling your sessions with Mickey, I think that you, too, should have a counselor. So that you can remain objective, and it will help prevent you from becoming overburdened."

"With guilt?" she asked.

"For one thing."

"Are you volunteering?"

Powell smiled and set his pipe in the ashtray. "I'd be glad to help. I've known Tom Horton for a good many years, and I would be happy to do anything to help his family."

"It's settled then. I'll go now. When Bill gets here, tell him I'll be right back. This should only take a couple of minutes."

"Good luck. I'll call the guards and tell them to let you into his room."

"Thanks."

Laura walked back down the stark hallway and waited for the guard to open the door to Mickey's room. She found him still lying on his bed and staring up at the ceiling, a satisfied smile playing on his lips. He looked up when she walked in.

"Hi, Mickey. I'm back."

Swinging his feet to the floor, Mickey eyed her. "Alone?"

"For now." Pulling the chair up next to the bed, she met his eyes and smiled at him. "I'm glad to be here, Mickey. I've missed you and worried about you. I've always wanted you to be happy. I hope you know that."

"That's all I've ever wanted for you, too."

"Then let's try to help each other. I just told Dr. Powell that I'm going to start coming for your therapy sessions, if that's what you still want."

"More than anything," he said.

"I'm glad you're taking what Bill told you so well. It wasn't easy for him. He loves you and cares about you, Mickey. He's never wanted to hurt you—ever."

"Our only problem is that we both fell in love with the same woman. I guess I can't blame him for that."

Laura blushed lightly, and extended her hand toward Mickey. "I'm going to help you, Mickey. We're going to get though this. Okay?"

He took her hand in his. "You don't know how much this means to me. I don't think I can make it without your help."

"I'll be right here, Mickey. I won't fail you."

As Laura said good-bye and turned to leave, Mickey watched her. "Thanks, Laura." *I've got you right where I want you.*

"I'm sorry about last night," Julie said, meeting Don at the door and grabbing her coat. "I was lousy company."

"I understand," he said, touching her cheek. "You had a bad shock. But tonight's going to be better. Right?"

"I promise." She forced a laugh, though she still felt sick inside. Just the thought of Doug and Kim together made her miserable. She'd suggested that she and Don see a movie; she had to do something, anything, to get Doug out of her mind. Even though she'd broken up with him days ago, her heart still ached when she imagined him holding Kim. . . .

"Are you sure you want to go out?" Don was still standing in the doorway, his eyes dark with concern.

"Of course I do! And we'd better hurry." Telling herself that she *didn't* love Doug Williams, she breezed out to Don's convertible and climbed into the passenger seat. "Tonight, we're going to have fun! Why don't you let down the top?" she said as he backed out of the drive.

"Are you out of your mind? It's barely above freezing."

She tossed her head, her dark hair flying free. "Oh, don't be such an old fuddy-duddy!"

"That, lady, is a challenge I can't ignore." Cranking open the top, he laughed.

Cold air rushed into the car and caught in Julie's hair, making it billow away from her face. Her blue eyes were bright, her cheeks pink from the bite of the wind. "This is great!"

"This is crazy, that's what this is!"

He pulled into the parking lot, and groaned when he saw the crowd at the theater. "Look at the size of that line!"

"A popular show," Julie murmured. "I had no idea. It's been out for more than a month. I thought the crowds would've thinned out by now."

"Guess again." Don took her hand and escorted her across the street. "It must mean it's good. So let's just relax and get in line. We've got the whole night." Slipping his arm around her waist, he kissed her cheek. "Strike that last comment from the record," he teased. "We've got the rest of our lives together!"

Julie snuggled into his arms, and they huddled together against the early evening chill. As the line moved and they slowly inched around the corner of the building, Julie glanced ahead, and suddenly felt as if she wanted to die. There, some fifteen feet ahead of them, were Kim and Doug—she, small and clinging, her dark hair gleaming, and he, holding her arm as if he'd loved her forever. Maybe he always had.

Don felt Julie stiffen and followed the path of her gaze. "Wouldn't you know?" He shook his head and turned his back on the offending couple.

Julie squared her shoulders. Doug wasn't going to ruin her evening. Not again. "We'll just have to make the best of it and forget about them, Don. Right?"

"Right." He gave her a heartfelt squeeze. "That's my girl."

So why didn't the words sound perfect? She forced a smile, but whenever Don wasn't watching her, she slid glances at Doug and Kim, fighting down the gnawing feeling of betrayal burning in her stomach.

Ahead of them, waiting for the line to move, Kim glanced over her shoulder to see how far the line had stretched. Her eyes clashed with Julie's, and she couldn't suppress a smile. Saying nothing to Doug, she only nestled closer to him, wrapping herself in his arms. "Brrrrr. I'm getting cold. Hold me tight, Doug."

His arm tightened around her. "How's that?"

"Much better." Standing on her tiptoes, she planted a kiss on his cheek, simultaneously sliding a glance toward the back of the line.

Julie's face drained of color. She tried desperately to fight back her jealousy, but failed. No matter how hard she tried to deny it, she knew she still loved Doug and would for the rest of her life. Loving Doug would be her cross to bear.

"Something wrong?" Don asked, seeing the lines etching across her brow.

The lie slipped out easily. "I'm not feeling very well. Maybe it's just the cold. I'll probably be okay once we get inside."

"Well, at least we're moving again. It shouldn't be long now."

She smiled up at him and tried to concentrate on the handsome lines of his face. He was good-looking and strong, charming and successful. But he wasn't Doug.

When they finally entered the theater, Don volunteered to wait in the concession stand line while Julie went to the restroom. "A large popcorn and a medium diet soda, right?" he asked.

"That'll be great. I'll be right back to help you carry it."

She entered the ladies' lounge and gazed at her reflection in the mirror. Her eyes looked positively dead, her shoulders slumped. "You're an idiot, Julie Anderson," she told the woman staring back at her. "A stupid, lovesick idiot!" She put on some lipstick and colored her cheeks and then forced a smile to her lips. "I can't let them do this to me. I'm going to make Don happy! Damn it, I'm through letting Doug ruin my life!"

But when she reentered the lobby, it only took one glance to destroy her composure. Doug was standing only a few feet away, with Kim still hanging on him, and as his blue gaze met Julie's, her heart began to pound.

Doug saw the look in Julie's eyes, and knew he was hurting her. But he couldn't look away.

"What is it, darling?" Kim asked.

"Nothing."

But Kim had caught sight of Julie, too, seen her pained expression. And when she glanced swiftly up at Doug, the sorrow in his eyes was unmistakable. "You're using me to get back at her, aren't you?" Kim whispered, feeling a stab of pain.

Doug sighed. "I wish I could lie to you."

Kim swallowed against the urge to scream and cry. "It's all right. I'll play along," she said, forcing a smile and knowing that Julie couldn't hear her.

"You don't have to."

"I want to, Doug. For you!" But deep in her heart she knew that she was playing for keeps.

Julie turned and stepped quickly through

the crowd, trying to ignore the pain in her heart. She found Don but couldn't pretend any longer that everything was fine.

"Here's your drink—are you all right?" he asked, concerned.

"No . . . I'm afraid I'm feeling worse. I thought I could rally myself once we got inside, but I think I might be coming down with something," she lied, hating herself for it. "I've got a terrible headache and my legs feel weak. If you want to stay, I could call a cab—"

"Don't be ridiculous. I brought you; I'll drive you home. If you're sure it's what you want."

"I think if I just lie down and rest, I can fight this off."

"I hope so." But the seed of doubt had been planted in his mind. "I don't suppose this has anything to do with seeing Doug and Kim?"

Julie winced, but shook her head. "Oh, no, Don. I couldn't care less what they do anymore. Don't start doubting me again. I'm sure it's probably just that bug that's been going around, the twenty-four-hour flu."

He helped her outside and sat her down on a bench. "You wait here. I'll bring the car around." He looked deep in her eyes and saw how worn she looked. Dropping down next to her, he put his arm around her shoulders. She was shaking. No matter what the cause, he had to take care of her. "Okay. I'll get you home and tuck you in, and we'll see how you are tomorrow. Maybe we can do this Friday night?"

"That would be great. You know how much I wanted to see this show. Now, don't be ridiculous. I'm perfectly capable of making it to the car."

He helped her to the convertible and put the top up. "This was probably what did it, you know—that harebrained idea of riding around with the top down."

"Maybe," she whispered, before lapsing into silence and trying not to think about Doug and the fact that just a few days ago he'd proposed to her.

Once inside her house, Don made her a cup of tea and tucked her into bed before giving her a peck on the cheek.

"I don't deserve you," she whispered.

"Probably not, but you're stuck with me. I'll call you in the morning." And then he was gone.

Left to herself, Julie grabbed a pillow and hugged it close to her chest. "What am I going to do?" she whispered, thinking of Doug's profile and his wintry blue eyes. "Why can't I rid myself of that man once and for all?"

The hours ticked by and she tossed and turned in her bed. No matter what she tried, she couldn't get comfortable. She couldn't drive the image of Doug with Kim from her mind. Were they together—sharing a bed?

"Damn that man! He's playing games with me, I know it. I hate him! I hate him! I hate him and I love him!"

Miserable, she got up and went down to the kitchen to make some more tea. Moonlight streamed in through the window, illuminating the room, and she remembered all the moonlit nights she'd spent with Doug. "I can't do this," she told herself aloud. "I can't keep torturing myself with thoughts of Doug. I've told Don that I'm going to marry him, and that's that."

She tried to concentrate on Don and all he stood for. She knew that he worshipped the ground she walked on. She knew he would always be there for her . . . loyal, trustworthy, honest, helpful. *Just like a boy scout!*

She stared out at the winter night, and knew that she had to make a choice. One man or the other. They'd both proposed, and she knew that they both loved her. Finally, she reached a decision. She knew what she had to do.

Her heart hammering, she reached for the kitchen phone and dialed the number by memory.

A groggy male voice answered.

"Hi—it's . . . it's Julie."

"I know who it is." He sounded surprised, but pleased to hear from her.

"Look, I've been going out of my mind the past few days, and . . . and I think we should just put the past behind us. Why don't we pack our bags and run away tonight and get married?" she said in a rush. "Let's just forget everything else, and do what we both know is right!"

He sounded both shocked and delighted. "You're sure?"

"Yes! I don't want to hassle with anything else, or wait another minute. Sometimes I feel there are so many outside pressures that we'll never wind up doing what we both know we should. I love you, you know I do. And you love me. That's all that matters. Please. Come and get me!"

The silence on the other end of the line seemed deafening. Julie counted her heartbeats. *Please say yes*, she silently prayed, knowing her life was about to be changed forever.

You can now order previous titles
of *Soaps & Serials*® Books by Mail!

Just complete the order form, detach, and send together
with your check or money order payable to:

Soaps & Serials®
120 Brighton Road, Box 5201, Clifton, NJ 07015-5201

Please circle the book #'s you wish to order:

(A) The Young and The Restless	1 2 3 4 5 6 7 8 9 10 11 12 13 14
(B) Days of Our Lives	1 2 3 4 5 6 7 8 9 10 11 12 13 14
(C) Guiding Light	1 2 3 4 5 6 7 8 9 10 11 12 13 14
(D) Another World	1 2 3 4 5 6 7 8 9 10 11 12 13 14
(E) As The World Turns	1 2 3 4 5 6 7 8 9 10 11 12 13 14
(F) Dallas™	1 2 3 4 5 6 7 8 9 10 11 12 13 14
(G) Knots Landing™	1 2 3 4 5 6 7 8 9 10 11 12 13 14

Each book is $2.50 ($3.50 in Canada).
Total number of books
circled_____ × price above = $ _____

Sales tax (CT and NY residents only) $ _____

Shipping and Handling $ _____ .95

Total payment enclosed $ _____
(check or money orders only)

Name_____

Address _____ Apt#_____

City_____ State _____ Zip _____

Telephone (_____)
         AREA CODE